FONTANA

FONTANA

•

Art Isberg

AVALON BOOKS
NEW YORK

© Copyright 2002 by Art Isberg
Library of Congress Catalog Card Number:
2002090729
ISBN 0-8034-9550-1
All rights reserved.
All the characters in this book are fictitious,
and any resemblance to actual persons,
living or dead, is purely coincidental.
Published by Thomas Bouregy & Co., Inc.
160 Madison Avenue, New York, NY 10016

PRINTED IN THE UNITED STATES OF AMERICA
ON ACID-FREE PAPER
BY HADDON CRAFTSMEN, BLOOMSBURG,
PENNSYLVANIA

This book is dedicated to all American Indians who
fought for their way of life,
the rule of the natural world, and a spirit embodied in
the land they knew and loved.

Chapter One

The Chase

The Ute chief Dull Knife and half a dozen braves had tied their ponies off in a stand of white-barked quaking aspen, then began hunting quietly on foot along a pine-studded ridge looking for deer. Up here at over 5,000 feet in the great backbone that would someday be named the Rocky Mountains, the fresh spring air was still but sharp, the brilliant sun of mid-April bright, illuminating the high country and everything in it with crystal clarity.

A short time later, the chief caught a subtle movement of gray and white ghosting through a small opening up ahead, signaling his men with a short, bird-like whistle then pointing at the deer still head down feeding as they moved. He held up three fingers then stabbed them right with a circling gesture as the red men dispersed to trap the animals in the Indian noose he'd just signed.

When they'd closed into killing range undetected, Dull Knife picked out a fat doe, carefully lifting his bow and aiming the arrow at a spot just behind her dark shoulder, then began to let loose, when suddenly Little Wolf, off to the right along a knife-edged rim, whistled a sudden alarm that stopped the red men's advance as they turned to find him. In that same instant the deer caught a man scent and bolted for safety scattering away with crashing "thump-thumps" and were gone.

When they converged, their eyes followed Little Wolf's pointed rifle barrel down the steep drop-off to the tiny figure of a lone rider slowly coming their way. The rider was no Indian but a white man, and obviously a foolish one to come here into the stronghold of the Utes so far from the safety of his own people, their many guns, and even the horse soldiers that rode farther to the south.

Dull Knife spoke quickly in low tones, his finger tracing the ambush plan in the air. Only a moment more and his men were moving downhill to take up positions alongside the elk trail their prize was riding on, and when they reached it, the first thing they noticed was the strange horse the white man rode, a big animal mostly white but dotted with large, black blotches. The brave who became owner of such a fine and unusual animal would be the envy of all others, not to mention furtive glances of young girls back in camp several miles away. Yes, this stranger's clothes, weapons, and scalp held great value, but nothing compared to the animal he was riding as each jockeyed to be first to get a clean shot and kill him.

But the lone white man was not as unaware of the possibility of trouble as he seemed, for he'd known he was in Ute country and had been keeping a sharp eye out for trouble ever since he left the grassy plains and rode into first timber. It was a chance he was willing to take for many reasons just as he'd done other dangerous things in his life for a man only thirty years of age, like scouting for the Sixth U.S. Cavalry along the Staked Plains many miles south fighting the savage Comanche, spending two summers down in Texas Territory buffalo hunting, slaughtering the great, brown, humped beasts until the barnyard smell of them filled his nostrils with revulsion, and the endless crack of big bore rifles finally swore him off killing for killing's sake.

Now he just wanted to leave what passed for "civilization," even out here on the western frontier, to spend a summer or maybe two living high up in the fastness and solitude of the magical chain of mountains that literally split a continent in half. He'd do some trapping, a little hunting to keep body and soul together, but mostly he just wanted to be alone to reassess his life and try to heal the soul-wrenching loss of loved ones murdered by three men he could never find, on their small farm they'd once all called home nearly a thousand miles back east, that was burnt to the ground. Never a day passed when he did not think of Jenny, his lovely wife, and his two young daughters Katie and Kathleen. Would his tattered soul ever be able to rest? He'd hoped the high country might give him some relief.

Just as he neared the wooded bend in the trail, he saw a sudden quick movement off in the distance. Instantly, he wheeled the big Appaloosa left, kicking him straight downhill into dog-hair timber at a breakneck run followed by a barrage of arrows rattling through timber around him as he streaked lower. His quick move caught the red men off guard and now they had to run for their ponies giving the lone rider precious minutes to get even farther down into dark timber. Dull Knife shouted orders for three of his warriors to take a short cut as the rest leaped on their horses and sped after the white man, yelling a killing cry as they kicked away.

Well down in thick pines, the white man whipped his powerful stud on with reckless abandon, for he knew full well that this was one race he had to win or die! They crashed through dead limbs and popping branches, leaping boulders and downfall trees until slowly, minute by agonizing minute, he could feel the big horse under him begin to tire, lungs heaving for oxygen, saliva flying from its open mouth as he whipped it harder and harder to stay ahead. Where was the bottom? How far down was it? If they could just reach it they might have a chance on a flat out run, as he dug the short leather whip deeper and deeper into flesh forcing, willing the big horse to stay on his feet and continue its murderous charge.

Then at last a dim halo of light grew below and the slope moderated slightly as he saw the first diamond twinkle of sunlight reflecting off the tinkling creek and moments later they burst out pulling to a skidding stop as he tried to decide which way to go. That was answered instantly when three Utes came steaming around the bend downstream barely a hundred yards away immediately opening up with their arrows as they pounded closer, and he jerked the appaloosa around again thundering upstream in a spray of flying water.

The big horse seemed to get a second wind as he took a quick look over his shoulder then ducked low, man and animal weaving back and forth across the small watercourse and arrows whined around them. Maybe he'd outrun them after all if they could just keep to open ground and out of timber. Then suddenly something slammed into the side of his head dealing a tremendous blow that rocked him violently as he fought to stay in the saddle. Everything began to blur and the unstoppable sensation gripped him that he was falling, falling, until finally he fell from the saddle crashing into the creek smothering for air. His world turned cold, black, and silent.

A long time later he stirred, barely aware of strange images and muffled voices moving over the top of him, his first coherent thought wondering if he was in heaven or hell? Then the pain came roaring back in a tidal wave so intense he thought it would kill him as he tried to cry out for help but could not, writhing on the cold hard ground feebly trying to bring a hand up to the wound on his blood-caked face, but could not.

Slowly, he realized his hands and feet were

bound to something driven hard into the earth and spread eagled, a shudder of cold creeping up his body stripped completely naked as he tried to call out again but only ended in a gargled moan. Then the hazy shadows turned into one barking out a single order and a moment later a cascade of icy water rained down nearly drowning him as he sputtered and twisted trying to catch his breath. But the water washed the blood from his eyes so he could finally see the circle of brown faces staring down at him, braves, women and children, as though he were a specimen in a jar.

Dull Knife stepped back motioning for someone to come up pointing down at him as he tried to speak before they killed him right where he lay.

"Where . . . am I?" He finally choked out the words. "Does . . . anyone . . . understand me? Someone help?"

But no one answered until a young woman stepped up staring down on him, her dark eyes framed by long, straight black hair that ran to her shoulders.

"My chief . . . Dull Knife wants to know . . . why you came here into our . . . land? He wants to know . . . how many white men came . . . with you, and where they . . . are?"

Stunned that anyone could actually speak

English, he lay there for a moment before trying to answer, eyes locked on the woman as he tried to compose his thoughts and catch his breath, for he knew that what he said now could spell the difference between an instant death or maybe a chance to live a few moments longer.

"There are no others . . . I came alone, and I came in peace. I wish to fight no one. How could . . . I, one man by myself? Could you please give me a drink of . . . water, please?"

She turned to the chief speaking quietly and after a moment he answered her with a terse grunt and she looked back down, her eyes slowly running the full length of his body trying to hide her curiosity.

"Dull Knife says . . . only a fool or . . . liar, would come into our land alone. He says, he does not be-lieve you and is sending out scouts now to . . . kill those that rode with you. Once this is done . . . he will . . . kill you too."

"I'm telling you the truth, for God's sake. There are no . . . others. He'll see that for himself. Tell him again. I do not lie. Now, can you give me a drink . . . please?"

Again she relayed the conversation and the chief stared back without blinking then said something turning away as she knelt beside him lifting a small reed bowl to his lips. He sucked in the icy liquid greedily until he began choking again, turning his head away, coughing out the excess. As he did he saw two dozen warriors mount up while Dull Knife gave them their orders, then rode out of camp at a breakneck pace, and he turned back to the woman.

"I'm frozen nearly stiff . . . can you give me something, anything to cover me . . . ask him?"

Again she turned to the Ute leader relaying the request then back to Fontana.

"Dull Knife says you will need noth-ing, because he will . . . kill you before the sun sleeps today."

"But you've got to tell him I . . . I . . . speak the truth. Make him understand . . . you've GOT TO!" He collapsed, tears running down his bloody face.

She started to try again but the chief ordered her to stop and move away and she immediately obeyed as the white man tried to yell after her but couldn't muster the strength, and the other Indians gathered there turned and left too.

Later, a few camp dogs tiptoed close, bristling and growling at the repugnant smell of this strange kind of man, but eventually even they too, left. Then a young boy no more than six or seven years old came slowly toward him and stopped, staring down, suddenly swinging a short stick down between his legs again and again until Kyle screamed out in pain and the boy's mother came running to pull him away.

Hours dragged by agonizingly slow as the sun sank lower into the tree tops then out of sight, and the evening haze of blue completely enveloped the Ute camp in plunging temperatures. Shivers wracked Kyle's body and try as he might he could not stop them. By full dark he was moaning out loud, frozen it seemed to the very depths of his soul, when suddenly he heard the hoofbeats of approaching ponies, twisting to strain at the thongs watching the search party of Utes ride in.

Dull Knife came out of his lodge talking for several moments before they all went back inside. Would they kill him now no matter what, like some pitiful dirty animal that didn't deserve to live? Maybe it would be a slow, torturous death most red men were famous for, but either way he knew he'd never live til dawn even if they just left him staked down there until tomorrow. He had nothing left, he was done for, groggy from loss of blood, dying of thirst, already nearly frozen to death.

Then the red men exited the lodge and started for their prize possession, gathering around him as the chief uttered orders and the braves scattered for a moment returning with firewood. But the blaze they set wasn't to warm him but only give enough light to keep him under surveillance. That done, they staked two mongrel dogs, one on each side as sentries, and satisfied with their efforts returned to their lodges. Slowly into the night, the fires finally burned down to just glowing pools of pulsing red then blinked out as night threw its icy cloak over the dying man.

He shook so violently that his teeth rattled in his mouth and breathing only came in short uncontrollable gasps. Where was death? Why didn't it come and take him? He was ready now, in fact he welcomed its ghostly arrival. Anything would be better than this, freezing inch by inch as cold and hard as the stones he was staked over. He writhed at the restraints feebly, the dogs growling low, flashing white fangs, until he stopped. If there was a God up in that starry sky over his head, he prayed he take him. He had nothing left to live for, nothing left to resist over. He closed his eyes and visualized the black cloaked approach of the Grim Reaper, then drifted off into semi-consciousness.

Sometime during the middle of the night he jerked awake, dogs whining, suddenly aware that someone was close by him, but in the dark he couldn't tell who. The shadowy form spread a furry blanket over him without a word being said, and when he tried to speak, something was shoved into mouth. It was a piece of meat and he chewed at it hungrily like a drowning man sucks air, as the silent figure stood up and vanished back into the night.

Slowly the heavy blanket began to warm even his frozen body as he finished off the fat-laden meat and for the first time in many hours actually drifted back off into sleep still wondering who had helped him and why? Then, at last, the first rose sliver of dawn painted the eastern sky and his benefactor returned, but this time he could see it was the young interpreter, as she pulled the heavy robe off of him then knelt to offer a quick drink of something hot while whispering in his ear.

"I must not be seen here. Our scouts found noth-ing yesterday. May-be Dull Knife will let you live? Today he will decide when he sees you are still alive." Then she stood and was quickly gone.

When sunlight broke over camp and fires were rekindled, the chief exited his lodge wrapped in a long skin robe. A dozen braves joined him as they conversed for a moment then started toward Fontana, whose shivers had returned in earnest, but when the Ute leader saw that the white man was actually still alive he registered a certain surprise across his usually stoic face, then ordered the woman be brought there.

"Dull Knife says . . . our scouts found no other white men. He says he will let you live . . . but he takes your guns, saddle, and horse. You must leave here on foot . . . to go back to your pe-ople. If you return he will have you killed on sight. He says that if you died last night he would have known you did not speak the truth."

Kyle tried to answer but couldn't, still wracked by his frozen body as they untied then dragged him to his feet only to immediately collapse back in a heap, his hands and feet numb and stiff. Again they yanked him up, a brave on each side half dragging, half stumbling across the camp toward the young woman's lodge where they threw him back down and he tried crawling for the entrance but went face down again as she came up to help.

"My chief says I can give you some-thing to eat and you may rest a little before you go. I am the only one here who speaks your language . . . so I must tell you how to leave. Come inside quickly now before he changes his mind."

Within the lodge, the warmth of a fire and thick, fur robes spread across the floor were so luscious that he collapsed face down while she covered him up. In moments he drifted into sleep as she kneeled next to the strangest man she'd ever seen, half frozen, beaten down in mind and spirit, yet there was something about him that fascinated her. Was it because he was the first white man she'd ever seen, his indomitable will to live against all odds, she really wasn't sure. But certainly this man of light hair like summer grass, green eyes that matched the stones of tinkling creeks, and body hair where she'd never seen it before on Ute men all held her focus. Why would such a man come alone to the mountain stronghold of her people? What would drive him to leave the smoky, log villages of whites she'd heard about with their noisy ways and filthy habits? Maybe she'd have enough time to ask him herself but not now, not as his aching body tried to get some relief from what they'd put him through.

Late that afternoon Kyle awoke with a cry, jerking up on both elbows as he tried to remember the terror chasing him. It took a moment to remember where he was, then he sank back down in the furry blanket as it all came flooding back. He was ALIVE, somehow his life had been spared just when it seemed he would surely die. He rolled over looking at the smoldering fire pit then along the far wall where packs and provisions were stacked. He was thirsty, bone-dry thirsty when he spied a reed bowl on the far side and began crawling toward it. He rolled over on his back pouring the wonderful liquid into his mouth. Just then the tent flap pulled back and the woman stepped in to peer down at him totally naked, and he instantly dropped the bowl and rolled for the protection of covers staring at her through his whiskery face.

"I did not . . . know you were a-wake." She said evenly, closing the flap behind her and kneeling across from him. "Do you . . . feel bett-er now after a rest?"

"Yes, I do, and I know I have you to thank for it, especially the robe and food you brought me last night. I wouldn't have made it if you hadn't done that. You saved my neck for sure, I'm not sure why, but I'm awfully glad you did. I don't even know your name."

"I am called, Quiet Moon in your white man's tongue. And you?"

"My name is Kyle, Kyle Fontana. I guess I've got so many questions to ask I don't really know where to start, but the first one would be how did you ever learn to speak such good English? From what little I know no one else here can."

"My mother was a . . . white woman. She was tak-en in a raid far from this place on a ranch where she used to live. Dull Knife our chief had a brother called Spotted Elk. He took her for his woman and she bore him a daught-er. I am that daught-er, but she died when I was still only a young girl. She told me once that she had an older broth-er, but he must have died too. My father, Spotted Elk, was killed in a fight with the Cheyennes not long after my mother went to the Spirit World. Then Dull Knife took me in with his fam-ily and raised me until I was old enough to have my own lodge."

"Well, how old do you think you are, do you really know?"

"No, not for sure, but I am woman enough to take care of myself . . . maybe nine-teen or twenty seasons old?"

"Do you remember your mother's family name, or anything else she told you?"

"She was never allow-ed to say it, but she told me it was some-thing like Rose . . . or Roose. Her white name was Izetta, but the Utes would not let her use it. You see, if a warrior takes a white woman her name changes to a tribal one and she can never say the other again or she will be beaten."

For several moments they looked at each other in complete silence as Kyle, up on both elbows now, studied this most unusual woman, thinking about the strange set of circumstances that had brought him here and the even stranger story of her life. Was it fate, bad or good luck he found himself in the middle of a Ute village where his life was in danger at every moment, yet shielded by Quiet Moon? Suddenly he had an idea so bizarre that even he had to rethink it before he spoke, but if fate was his companion then he'd play out the hand for all it was worth.

"I want to ask you to do something that might seem strange and even dangerous. Would you do it for me?"

"What would you ask?"

"I want you to go to your chief and tell him . . . I want to stay here in his village and spend the summer learning the ways of the Ute people. He knows now I told the truth and that I'm alone. I did not come to make war. I came to learn the ways of nature, what your people call the Great Spirit. I wanted to learn to live in peace and harmony with the land, to take only the animals I needed to eat, and some furs to trade when I leave a year or two from now. I meant to live alone, but now that I'm here I can learn much more from you and your people if they will let me. Will you ask?"

"Dull Knife will not let you stay. No white man is his friend. He does not trust the white eyes, and has already said you must go soon as you can walk, or die."

"Yes, I know that, but if you take me to him and tell him my words maybe he will listen to you. I can even show him how my rifle kills far beyond any arrow, how to make bullets from iron that runs like water over a fire, and how to make fire from my steel starter. All these things can make him and his warriors stronger against his enemies. In return he can show me the ways of your world and by summer's end both of us will be better off for learning such things from each other. Will you do it, will you try for me?"

She gazed at the white man without answering, puzzled he would make such a strange request just when he'd won his freedom, then turned to hand his clothes to him as she got to her feet.

"Here are your things and mocc-asins. Dull Knife has taken the rest of them, your guns, knife, and horse. Let me think on what you have asked. It may be too dangerous for me to speak of such things. I'll give you my answer to-morr-ow."

"Please try to understand, Quiet Moon. I am not like other whites your people may have come into contact with. I mean what I say and speak from the heart."

She stood a moment longer then exited the lodge as Kyle laboriously pulled on his clothes then tied the knee-high moccasins up. If she'd just ask he knew he had a chance with her on his side. Then he got to his feet and stepped outside squinting into the bright sun, steadying himself on the lodge frame as several women nearby turned to stare at him and even a pair of mounted braves twisted on their ponies to glare at him in contempt, uttering insults under their breath.

The warming sun never felt better and the longer he stood there soaking it up the more his strength slowly seemed to return. Finally, he sat and closed his eyes resting his head in both hands, rethinking the bizarre events that had brought him here. By all rights he should be dead. Only hours ago he was as good as dead, yet now he was alive asking for the chance to live with the very same people who'd captured and were ready to kill him. If only Quiet Moon could convince the chief, that's all he asked, if only somehow she could.

When he looked up again she was walking steadily across the village toward him as he studied her purposeful stride and beautiful form. Reaching him she knelt down, her dark eyes locked on his as she spoke.

"I have al-ready talked with Dull Knife. I

told him of your re-quest. I told him your heart was true, that you wish to learn the ways of our people, and that you speak the truth as he himself has seen. He will talk to you to-night around his fire."

"You've already seen him, not waited until tomorrow like you said earlier?"

"Yes, I felt it would be best to do so now when you are still weak and he is strong because of it. Tomorrow he would have made you leave and not given you the chance."

"Thank you, Quiet Moon." Kyle slowly got to his feet. "I owe you more than you'll ever know."

But she only turned and quickly entered the lodge without another word.

Chapter Two

Indian Summer

After eating that evening she took Kyle to Dull Knife's lodge, making the proper overtures while he stood outside waiting to be invited in. In a moment she was back beckoning him, the chief sitting by a small cooking fire, the play of light and shadow dancing across his emotionless face as he watched them enter. Behind him against the wall his wife and two grown daughters pulled their robes up nearly covering their faces as they peered alarmingly at the first white man they'd ever seen. Then Quiet Moon began to speak in low, respectful tones as Dull Knife's eyes locked on Fontana. When she'd finished he studied these strange white eyes a moment longer then answered in short, sharp words.

"Dull Knife says no white man can live like an Indian. He says you are too soft . . . too used to your white man's ways and easy lives in smoky, far away log villages."

"Tell your chief I know it will not be easy, but I admire him and his people and want to learn to live like them. I came to these mountains to learn such things though I did not know I would find your people. I thought I would be alone, but now that I am here I ask for his help. Tell him I also have a Great Spirit that lives in me, and that spirit has told me to ask for these things. I do not wish to make him angry by disobeying his orders."

The red man listened intently then leaned slightly forward with a question of his own.

"My chief says if you wish to learn the Ute ways then are you also ready to battle our enemies like the Cheyenne or others?"

"Yes, if need be I would, though I did not come here to fight anyone. I've seen enough of death already, both red and white man."

Dull Knife sat back never taking his eyes off Fontana and posed another question.

"He asks, what if we fought a-gainst other whites . . . would you still raise your hand in blood?"

Kyle knew the old warrior was trying to trap him in his own words, and now he had to think very carefully before answering.

"Tell Dull Knife that if there was no other way, and my people were clearly in the wrong, then yes, I would defend him and his people."

The chief's hand went slowly to his face as if to wipe away something as he thought about Kyle's reply, then he spoke only a few words, dismissing his visitors with a small wave of his hand.

"Tomorrow he will tell you his answer. Now, we must go."

As promised the next morning well after sun up they were summoned back to his lodge, but this time they met out front. After a short conversation Quiet Moon turned to Kyle.

"Dull Knife says he will let you stay a-mong his people to see if your words match your deeds. But, you will not be gi-ven back your weap-ons, traps, or horse. You can pick a new one from our herd. He has already given your spotted horse to the brave who captured you."

"But, without my weapons I cannot even defend myself or even hunt. How am I supposed to survive like that? I'm a man not a woman who stays here in camp all day. And besides, no one else but me can ride Snow Ball. He's no good to any of Dull Knife's braves, tell him that."

Within moments the chief summoned up a fierce looking warrior pulling Kyle's horse behind him, then ordered him up on its back, turning to the white man talking through Quiet Moon.

"He says his brave has no trouble riding your animal, and he thinks your words must be false."

"Then tell him to have this man try and ride away."

Kyle nodded, and in a flash the red man kicked the big appaloosa forward on a short run until he put two fingers to his mouth and sent out a short, shrill whistle skidding the animal to so sudden a halt that the Indian lost his seat and flew over its neck, landing on the ground in a cloud of dust. Dull Knife turned to look at the white man with a mixture of surprise and mirth. Then he spoke quickly and turned away.

"The chief says you may keep your horse, but he will still keep your weapons until he is sure you can be trusted."

"Did he say where I will sleep?" Kyle asked.

"Yes, you will stay in my lodge be-cause I am the only one here who speaks your tongue, but when the autumn moon rises in the east you must be able to speak our tongue so he may talk to you of other things that only men can say to each other, and not through a woman's mouth."

And so Fontana's lessons began in the days and weeks ahead, at first limited to duties around the village where he was kept under the distrusting eye of one or more braves who made it crystal clear through gestures and language that they did not like him or the duty they'd been given. Later, they began letting him ride out with scouting, then hunting parties lasting two or sometimes three days, and it was on one of these that he nearly lost his life and what finally convinced Dull Knife to return his long barreled rifle, pistol, and cartridges.

He was out with half a dozen braves hunting for game when one day near high sun they returned to their temporary camp to eat and rest, two fat mule deer hanging from a meat pole. After eating Kyle decided to walk downhill to a small creek to drink, passing through a thick stand of pines to reach it. He knelt and scooped up a handful of icy water bringing it to his lips but found himself looking straight into the face of an enormous grizzly bear coming through trees across the creek and obviously following his nose on the wafting aroma of fresh venison.

When the huge bore finally saw him crouching there it pulled to a stop and stood up on its hind legs trying to make out exactly what he was, and in that same instant Kyle leaped to his feet, running back uphill yelling a warning as he gained ground with the bear charging across the creek right on his heels! When he burst into camp the red men were already scattering, running for their horses even though they did not understand a word of English. His scream of "Bear! Bear!" was warning enough. Just as they leaped on their ponies the big grizz came barreling into the clearing popping branches with coughing roars as they frantically kicked away.

When they reached camp the next morning without their venison, Dull Knife heard the story and gave Fontana back his weapons. Then he turned to Quiet Moon, uttering a few words before walking away without waiting for an answer.

"What did he say?" Kyle asked.

"He wants to know why you did not whistle and stop the bear as you did your horse?" The briefest smile tightened her lips then vanished quickly as it had come, but Kyle's did not.

With all his gear back he now began trapping in earnest as the Utes showed him many places where beaver, muskrat, and sometimes otter could be found, and his cache began to grow. And slowly, one word or phrase at a time, he also began his lessons on speaking the Ute tongue, something he picked up surprisingly fast with the woman to teach him nearly daily. On some of his trapping forays he took her with him, though their relationship always remained purely platonic, her actions showing no personal interest in him. She'd been instructed to teach him many things and that's exactly what she meant to do, even though on more than one occasion Kyle began to wish he could break that arm's length barrier of hers and get closer.

He'd watched her strong, young body moving under tanned buckskin each evening around the fire as she prepared something for them to eat, the dancing shadows of light and dark outlining her lovely figure. One evening when he laid his sleeping robe too close she quickly ordered him to move to the other side of the firepit and he did so without complaint, embarrassed at her quick rejection and resolved not to make the same mistake again.

Later that summer after he'd been out many times, Dull Knife told him of a place far to the south where mountains ran down into hill country and a large number of creeks, springs, and shallow lakes held many skins for trapping. He asked Quiet Moon if she knew of this place and she told him she did and would guide him there if he wished to go, but that sometimes it could be risky because Cheyenne warriors also came up from the farther south to hunt buffalo on the grassy plains just beyond the hills. Yet he still wanted to go.

"We will need two extra horses to pack our goods and your traps. And we will need a lodge to sleep in and cook. I have been to this land of many smokes twice before, but on-ly when we had many warriors with us, so we must be careful. It will take four suns to reach."

Two days later they were packed and ready to leave, standing before the chief's teepee as he talked to Kyle through the woman.

"Remember what I have said. That is not our land unless we go there in numbers. Even your white man's rifle can only fire one ball at a time. You must not let the Cheyennes find you for they would kill you and Quiet Moon would become their slave. Listen to what she tells you. Then you will return with many skins . . . and your hair too. Now go."

The long, winding trip down through the mountains was both exhilarating and glorious, each day rimming deep, blue canyons thick in tall timber, every night eating close to a small but friendly fire then crawling into their sleeping robes snug against the chilling mountain air. Then they rode into a mixed country of plateau lands with willow, alder, and still some pines, but where tumbling waters from high country coursed through sagebrush canyons before finally spreading out into a rolling land of grassy valleys and small lakes teaming with fur bearing animals. Here they set up their camp and pole teepee, on a slightly elevated piece of ground just above a big pond.

It didn't take long working in the warm sun for Kyle to strip off his buckskin clothes and work each day only in a loin cloth and buckskin boots just as the Utes did, but eventually he even abandoned the boots and wore only a small pair of moccasins that Quiet Moon made him, and a red bandanna tied around his forehead to keep sweat out of his eyes. She skinned and stretched the pelts on round willow frames to dry as their cache began to build.

One afternoon when he returned to camp he found her kneeling over the frames working in the hot sun but stripped down only to her short buckskin skirt without a top, sweat glistening off her body. At his approach she came to her feet turning to greet him, his eyes instantly falling on the lovely cups of bare, firm, upturned breasts ringed in darker brown tips. He tried not to stare but couldn't stop as she looked back at him unashamed.

"Have you not seen a woman before?" She broke his gaze.

"Well, yes . . . I have, but it's been . . . a long time, that's all. I'm just not used to seeing you look . . . like this."

"This is how we live, Ky-le. You should think noth-ing of it. I know it is not the white man's way but you no longer look like a white man either. Have you look-ed at your-self in the wa-ter?"

"No, I haven't really, but I know I've never been happier in years than these last two weeks since we left camp and came here. This is the kind of life I was looking for when I rode into the mountains, the kind of peace I need to heal many scars. Now, I believe I've found it. Can I ask you something . . . personal?"

She nodded, still standing hands on her hips studying his suddenly melancholy mood.

"When I was taken by your people did you really help me because Dull Knife ordered you to, or was there any other reason, maybe an interest?"

Her face never betrayed an answer and no answer passed her lips as she finally broke her stare and turned back to the pelts.

"We still have much work to do. It will not grow dark for a while longer, so you may check other traps."

But maybe by avoiding his question she'd already given Kyle the answer he sought, and now he turned away without pressing the issue any further.

Those first two weeks passed into three as furs mounted and both of them lived like children of the wild. After exhausting furs close by camp, Kyle began riding farther and farther out each day to new water, the lowlands remaining hot and sunny as summer advanced. But he also couldn't kid himself either about his even more powerful affection for Quiet Moon and how he couldn't wait each day to return to her then watch as she built the evening fire, prepared meals, then sat to eat across from each other often saying little or nothing at all as they just stared. Was she thinking the same thing he was thinking? How he wished he knew, but didn't dare ask. Then it was to bed and up again at dawn, the warming sun on his back as he worked, the whistle of a hawk high in the sky above him, on a life that never was better and one that he wished would last the rest of his days.

Late one afternoon as he drew near camp he suddenly saw the distant figures of riders sweeping down through trees, then Quiet Moon running for the teepee. Instantly, he dug his heels into Snow Ball on a thundering run across shallow flats, spray flying as a primeval yell came from his throat to turn the marauders away from her, and turn they did, two of the Indians immediately charging through the water straight at him two hundred yards away.

As they closed, Kyle hung low over his horse's neck and yanked the rifle up in one swift motion, cranking the hammer back leveling the barrel on the Cheyenne on his right as they came together, pulling the trigger and spilling the Indian backwards off his running pony with a bullet in his chest, and hitting in a geyser of spray. The second red man flashed by firing and missed, but Kyle did not turn to take him on, instead driving the big Appaloosa straight on for camp, Quiet Moon, and the third Cheyenne who'd just run into the teepee after her.

Now he heard a sudden gun shot just as he reached dry ground and leaped down running for the lodge, ripping the flap back, the empty rifle cocked in his hand like a club as the warrior staggered out backwards clutching his stomach from the pistol wound he'd suffered only to be hit full across the face with all the strength Kyle could muster and he collapsed in a bloody heap.

Inside, Quiet Moon was writhing on the robes, her hand clutching the feathered shaft of an arrow deeply embedded in her shoulder. She cried out in pain as he dropped down beside her trying to extract the wooden missile without success.

"That arrow's got to come out!" His voice was a fever pitch as he straddled her, pinning both shoulders with his knees, quickly unsheathing his belt knife and cutting off the shaft several inches above flesh.

"I'm sorry, Quiet Moon. There's no other way, that arrow's got to come out. Here, bite down on this." He picked up a small stick by the firepit, forcing it into her mouth, then placing the flat side of his knife blade on the bloody stub hesitating a moment as he raised his shoulders full up, tensed for what was to come, then shoved down fast with all his might forcing the razor-edged flint out her back as she screamed and twisted under him.

"Listen to me!" He rolled her over quickly cleaning the wound then wrapping it. "These Cheyennes will be back. These three were probably just a scouting party. We have to leave here quickly, and you'll have to ride on your own. If we ride double we'll never outrun them. There's no choice, you've got to hang on with everything you've got. Now let's go!"

He lifted her trembling body outside then rounded up their horses, steadying her in the saddle. A moment later they both kicked for timber and were swallowed up in deep shadows fleeing for their very lives.

Almost an hour later Kyle stopped just long enough to take a quick look back downhill making out the thin column of black smoke rising from their camp. The Cheyennes were burning it after taking anything they wanted, and now they'd come for them with every ounce of strength and cunning they possessed. He pulled up alongside the woman stroking her neck for a moment as she clung head down in the saddle, encouraging her to go on no matter what. Then they were off again climbing at a run.

When nightfall came he heard a small cry for help and turned to see Quiet Moon feebly pull her mount to a stop then slowly slide to the ground. In an instant he leaped off his horse and was beside her, lifting her in his arms as she tried to whisper to him.

"I can—not go on... you must, save... your-self. Ride for the vill-age. Go now... please, while you have the... chance."

Without answering he lifted her atop Snow Ball then climbed on behind, wrapping his powerful arms around her, kicking the big animal forward again, wondering how close the Cheyenne were behind them.

Sometime near dawn he stopped at a small spring, watering the horse and lifting a palm full of the icy liquid to her fevered lips, then unwrapping the bloody bindings and cleaning the wound as best he could before covering it back up, while the half delirious woman said nothing looking at him through glazed eyes.

They rode steadily most of that day with only jagged peaks still ahead as a compass guide, but finally even Kyle had to stop, carefully lifting her down then laying next to her in a shaded spot under pines.

"I've got to rest just a little, then we'll move on," he whispered, but she didn't respond at all. "Maybe just an hour or two then we'll leave." He wrapped his arms around her and was fast asleep in moments.

He awoke with a start sitting bolt upright as his hands dug frantically in the pine needles for the rifle, and the first streak of dawn painted the eastern sky. Good God, he'd slept all night! For a moment longer he didn't dare breathe listening for what had startled him but all he heard was the pounding of his own heart in his chest, then the raucous call of a blue jay high above them. Ever so carefully he extracted himself from Quiet Moon and stood looking around. Snow Ball stood head down quiet and still. Maybe it was nothing at all that startled him? Maybe it was just raw-edged nerves and a nightmare dream that they'd been captured that electrified him? But now it was time to get going again and he carefully awoke then got her to her feet and back atop the horse.

Late that afternoon while pushing through a particularly bad stretch of downed timber, he suddenly came across what looked like the remnants of an old horse trail and turned down it as it wound in and out of timber then out across several knife-edged ridges. When it got too dark to see he gave the animal its head, fighting to stay awake and keep both of them upright in the saddle, but in another hour he lost that battle and fell asleep with the woman locked in his arms until sometime later when Snow Ball stopped, snorting into the dark with distended nostrils, rousing him back to consciousness.

"What is it boy? Do you hear something?" He sat motionless for several more minutes before finally moving again as the Appaloosa quickened his pace across the fire-blackened bench then began angling down a steep hillside into what must be a valley. As they descended Kyle thought he caught just the faintest glow of dying campfires far below, and half an hour later he was sure of it as his spirits cautiously rose. But what if it wasn't a Ute camp? Maybe he'd blundered right into the Cheyenne again, and if that was the case this time he didn't stand a prayer of escaping with a played out horse and half-dead woman to keep in the saddle. But he had to take a chance. He had to pray this was help, and so he carefully urged the horse into a clearing close enough that he could see the dark outline of many teepees and finally called out for help.

Slowly, shadowy figures appeared from the lodges, then thankfully helping hands reached up to take the woman from him as he fought back his own fatigue sliding out of the saddle. Then Dull Knife was at his side trying to ask him questions but the one word he did understand was "Cheyennes," and now he knew enough. Kyle walked wearily toward his lodge and stumbled inside collapsing on a pile of warm furs. At last he could sleep in safety, and sleep he did all the way into the next afternoon.

When he awoke he lay there for a moment staring up at the crossed poles. Then he remembered the cruel events of the last several days and quickly pulled himself to his feet, going outside heading for the chief's lodge. Dull Knife came out speaking to him slowly so he could understand as much as possible, then gestured him inside. The young woman lay covered, the red man's wife and two daughters tending her, washing the jagged arrow wounds in some kind of milky liquid as she quivered in pain, her glazed eyes finally falling on Kyle as he knelt next to her.

"How are you doing—now that you've got some real help?" He tried to force a small smile as her hand slid out from under the covers to find his and hold it weakly, staring at him for several moments longer before trying to talk in a low, hoarse whisper.

"You... saved us... both, Ky-le. With-out... your strength... the Cheyenne would have... us." Her eyes closed again as she took in a long, slow breath.

"You're going to get well, Quiet Moon. You have to because no one else here can teach me all I still do not know. Even now I cannot tell Dull Knife everything that happened to us."

She lifted her hand to his lips touching them lightly as she spoke again.

"I... have..al-ready told... him. He understands... he says you... grow more like a... warrior each day. Our escape from... the Cheyenne proves it... to him. He say..."

"Don't try to talk anymore. Just rest now and regain your strength. There'll be plenty of time later for that. All that matters now is that you get the rest you need, then I'll come back tomorrow again, OK?"

He leaned down and kissed her lightly on the forehead, then stood and went back outside followed by the chief. The red man locked eyes with him then put his hand on his shoulder without saying a word, but Kyle understood exactly what it meant. He was accepted now nearly as one of the Utes, and by the most powerful man in all the Ute nation. It was a great honor, something he'd hoped for almost from the moment his life was spared. Now, if the woman he was obviously falling in love with would just pull through, if the healing herbs and natural powers of these people of nature really did work, then he might find a path for the rest of his life he never even dreamed possible.

Chapter Three

The Traders

In the weeks ahead Quiet Moon's raging fever slowly subsided and little by little the poison drained from her body as strength returned, but she would always carry the vicious scars of their near fatal encounter with the Cheyennes.

When she finally returned to her own lodge and Kyle, the two became closer than ever even though they still had not consummated their growing relationship with the ultimate act of love. Kyle's language skills grew good enough that she could speak to him only in her native tongue, which forced him to become even better, and Dull Knife could also see that this strange white man he'd taken in and his adopted daughter were on the brink of marriage Indian style.

When the two talked, the chief wanted to know why the white man continued to push into the valleys and mountains of the red man, what land they came from far away where the sun rose, and why they thought wherever they stood that they would own that land as their own? Although he tried to explain the best he could, it was lost on the mind of the Ute leader. Dull Knife also told him that he and his people did not want to fight the white man with his powerful rifles, and only wanted to be left alone to live in the vastness of their mountains and foothills as they always had. Yet, his advanced scout riding far to the south and sometimes east reported more whites than ever out on the plains slaughtering buffalo and even engaging the dreaded Cheyenne wherever they found them.

"Those white eyes are not like you, Fontana. They do not live in the heart of the Great Spirit as you have learned to do. They kill everything they see, and leave meat to rot on the ground for vultures to eat. I do not understand such things. Have they no mother to teach them better?"

Kyle could not explain these things either

and the result was that in the end the chief could only conclude all white men must be crazy mad for power over all they came in contact with, both Indians and the animals they depended on for their survival. Then he finished with a telling warning.

"If they come here into our mountains as they have below, there will be much trouble. I will stop them and many will die for that is the only thing they understand."

Slowly the months of summer slipped away as Kyle continued trapping and Quiet Moon's strength returned. By the first cool nights of fall his cache had grown to such large proportions that he proposed riding down out of the mountains to the nearest town or trading post. He was told the nearest was a place called Riverton, four days ride east and situated on the bend of a river called the Wind River, but Dull Knife didn't want him to go.

"Why do you need white man's money? It can buy you nothing you do not have here for the taking. When you are hungry you eat. When you need clothes you have a woman to make them. You have ponies and a lodge of your own now. I do not understand what more any man needs."

But he explained he was running low on gun powder and ball for both his rifles and pistols, and that he might also be able to buy some rifles that the Utes could learn to use, growing their own power not only among other tribes, but also any confrontation with whites should that ever take place. And he finished by telling him that he might also learn of any movements white men were making on the fringes of Ute country. But the old man still was not convinced.

"I have taken you into my lodge, but I do not want other white men to follow you here when you return. If you go they will ask you many questions. No good can come from it. Stay here Fontana. Stay where both you and I are safe from their ways. Those other white men will not change as you have."

"They will not follow me, I promise you that. I will tell no one of this place and no white man can make me. Trust me, Dull Knife, as you've learned to trust me all these months I've been here. Have I ever lied or failed you?"

He studied his friend a moment longer, then answered.

"It is not you I worry about. I know you are strong, but I worry about those as you once were yourself before you came here. If you do go remember this. Our land is sacred and meant only for our people. Any whites that try to follow you back will never leave these mountains alive. And if that happens many more whites will come looking for them and war will follow. Think on this before you decide."

"I will, Dull Knife, but I believe we can get what we need and return without the trouble you see. I will ride fast and straight without leaving a trail for anyone to follow. When I return, you and your men will have rifles such as mine and I will teach you how to shoot them, making you even more powerful than you are now. Think of the good that will bring."

When he told Quiet Moon of his plans she immediately wanted to make the journey with him, even though he tried to dissuade her with a warning.

"I've never been to Riverton, but I've been to other frontier towns before and I can tell you it's no place for a woman to be, not any kind of woman. Do you understand what I mean? I don't need you on this trip. I'm only going to trade then return quickly, that's all. If I had what I wanted I wouldn't go at all."

She came up face to face, her dark brown eyes penetrating his like she always did when she was determined to get her way, almost as if she could look into his very soul, her slender hands slowly clutching his buckskins, pulling him even closer.

"Ky-le . . . please listen to what I have to say and try to understand it. You know my mother was white woman, do you not? She was as white as you yourself are, but I know nothing of her ways or her people. I do not know how they live, how they act among their own, and this is the only chance I will ever get to see for myself. That's why I want to go with you, to see such things and no other reason. Please . . . take me with you. You know about the people you came from, but I only know half of myself."

He looked down on her sighing slightly, already shaking his head in defeat, wrapping both arms around her slender waist pulling her close.

"If you want to go that bad then I guess you can, but let me ask you one more question. Have you ever thought you might not like what you find down there?"

"That may be true, but let me learn that for myself, not by someone telling me."

"All right then, but remember what I said. This is not going to be as easy as you believe."

"I will not complain, I promise."

He leaned lower, kissing her lightly on the lips then straightening up as she studied him.

"Does it give you pleasure to put your mouth to mine?"

"Yes, great pleasure. It is our way of showing how much we love someone, by touching this way without speaking."

"Then I will learn to do it better so you know that I love you too in the same way."

She pulled his head down, wrapping both arms around his neck and holding him there as their lips met, working back and forth until both had to pull back to catch a breath.

"Is that better?" She asked, wide eyed.

"It was . . . much better, but now I think we'd better begin to get ready for the trip."

"You are already tired of doing it?"

"No, not tired, but I just think it would be better if . . . we did it maybe later. I like it, but sometimes it's better to wait."

It took several days to get the packs together and other trail goods plus food, then finally they led the four-horse string out of the village, stopping briefly at Dull Knife's lodge.

"I will be out with a hunting party for four suns, but remember what I have said. Do not let any whites follow you back. You will be back among your people, but they will not know you now. I have seen it in my dreams. You will be a stranger among them. Be careful,

Fontana. They are not your friends. Go now and return soon."

They swung their string east and south over the next five days, slowly descending the high ranges until finally reining to a stop late one afternoon and looking down at the blue veil of hazy smoke rising from the valley below, then the tiny dots of log buildings marking the town of Riverton encircled by the silver crescent that was the Wind River.

"There it is." Kyle dismounted, stretching his legs as Quiet Moon followed coming up beside him to gaze fixedly at the distant community.

"Will we ride there today?" she asked.

"No, there's no rush. Let's wait until morning, then we'll go down. The horses need a good night's rest and so do we. We'll camp up here tonight."

The next morning they loaded up and started down reaching the outskirts of town an hour later and riding down the muddy main street in single file as the few men already out stopped to stare at the strange looking white man, his Indian woman, and the two pack horses loaded with heavy goods. Once Kyle slowed to ask a gawker if there was a trading store, but for a moment all he could do was stare at Quiet Moon before he finally answered.

"There's Brady's . . . down there." His eyes finally went back to Fontana. "He's got a sign board out front."

At the end of the street they pulled to a stop and Kyle dismounted.

"Wait here while I go inside and get somebody. I won't be gone long."

He mounted the rough log steps and went inside while she slowly twisted in the saddle taking in everything in town including the whiskery faced men who began gathering around her staring as if they'd never seen a woman before.

Inside, Brady's was both dry goods, hardware store and a small bar situated near the back, walls lined with shelves stacked with dozens of items of every description. As he approached the bar he saw three men lounging in chairs over a half empty bottle of whiskey, one turning to eye him curiously as he came up, a rolled cigarette in one hand and a glass in the other.

"Yeah . . . what can I do for you?" He asked.

"Are you Brady?"

"That's right, just like it says on the sign out front. You must'a been in the hills a long time to be dressed like that!" He glanced at his pals, smiles wrinkling their hairy faces.

"I've come here for powder and bullet lead. Maybe some rifles too if you have them."

"Powder and lead, huh? Well, yeah, I've got plenty of both, probably more than you could haul in a freight wagon. But what have you got to trade for it, venison, elk meat, or something else I don't need?"

The three laughed again then Brady topped off their glasses, still eyeing Fontana.

"I've got furs. Beaver, otter, muskrat, all prime pelts. You want to do some business or just sit there emptying that bottle?"

"Furs?" Brady slowly turned full around in the chair. "This country around here's been pretty well trapped out, and what's left sure as hell ain't prime by any stretch of the imagination. I don't think you've got much to show me, mister."

"Well, you won't find out wearing that chair out. Do you want to take a look or not? If you don't I'll take them someplace else."

"Someplace else? Haaaa! There ain't another town around here for nearly a week's ride. But I'll take a quick look at what you're so proud of. C'mon, lead the way."

All three got up and followed Kyle outside where a small crowd had gathered around Quiet Moon, some even trying to get her to talk. Brady and his two pals eyed her up and down then looked at each other knowingly as Kyle untied a pack pulling out a thick beaver pelt and handing it to Brady. His eyes quickly narrowed as he ran his fingers through the luxurious fur.

"Is all this fur, both horses here?"

"That's right." Kyle nodded.

"And does it all look like this?"

"It does. Like I said, prime pelts."

"Where in hell did you find hides like this? It sure wasn't around here anyplace, I'll tell you that right now."

"Where isn't important. All I want to know is do you want to do some trading or not?"

"Well, yeah, if it's all this good. But I want to see the whole spread laid out. Why don't you bring your horses around back where we can unload it. Ah . . . is this your woman here, your wife, or something?"

"I'm not trading the woman, just these pelts."

"Sure, sure, that's fine. I was just wondering. We don't see too many woman of any kind around here Indian or not. If you don't mind me saying so, she's downright fetching, you're a lucky man, by God, to be traveling with someone like that. I don't mean no disrespect mind you, I was just surprised to see her out here just like the rest of these men. I thought you were traveling alone, but anyway let's get these horses around back. Buck, Zinky, you two come on and help."

Kyle mounted up and started the string around to the alley while the three men went through the store and once inside talked quickly among themselves.

"By God, that's the best looking woman I've seen since I left Saint Louis!" Zinky exclaimed. "Them squaws don't usually look anything like that, I'll tell you for sure. And she's no full-blooded Indian either, not by a long shot, and ridin' around with a white man to boot. I wonder how he pulled that off without losing his hair?"

"I'm not worrying about no female right now. I just want to get a good look at what he's got in the rest of those packs, because if it all looks that good he's working country I want to know about. I may have just found me a new partner." Brady laughed a con man's chuckle under his breath as they exited the back door.

An hour later everything had been unpacked as the proprietor walked around slowly, hands on his hips, studying the goods.

"Well, all right, mister, you've got yourself a deal. By the way, what's your name anyway?"

"Fontana, Kyle Fontana."

"OK Kyle Fontana. You live around these parts someplace or are you just passing through? I know pretty well everyone in this part of the country and I've never seen you before."

"No, I don't live around here but that's not important. I just want to trade for the goods I mentioned earlier, and I might also pick up a few things extra."

"What I'm trying to say, is are you coming back through here with more pelts anytime soon, say before the snow flies? You see, if I can depend on you to do so I can do a steady business with my supply people back east, the fur market being what it is. There's a few trappers working this part of the country but they aren't doing much, nothing like this. Maybe you and I could work out a "business" arrangement of some kind? You know, I'd supply you with whatever you need, and you'd bring your furs to me. That makes sense, doesn't it, and the . . . lady here, she might want something nice too. I mean, she looks just fine in buckskin, don't get me wrong, but you'd think she might like something a little frilly once in a while? By the way, does she understand anything we've said here, or just speak injun?"

Quiet Moon stared at Brady, then over his

two leering partners and back to Kyle who nodded ever so slightly.

"Yes, I under-stand every-thing you've said," she answered calmly. "And I even speak . . . in-jun too."

Brady's jaw dropped in disbelief before snapping back shut, trying not to show his surprise as he recovered.

"Why, that's real nice ma'am. I didn't mean no disrespect by asking." He forced a weak smile. "You and Mr. Fontana here are just full of surprises, aren't you?"

"Let's get down to business on a price." Kyle interrupted. "I want to be on my way back and out of here by nightfall."

"Back where?" Brady quickly countered hoping for an answer.

"Just back, that's all, now let's get on with it."

"For God's sake man. Why don't you give yourself and the woman here a break? Stay a day or two and rest your animals. You might find it a little interesting and we'd have time to work out a real good deal for both of us. Let the woman see what civilization looks like, it won't hurt her none. What's the rush?"

"I know what civilization looks like and so does she now. We didn't come here for that, now I want to settle up on a price."

Brady shrugged his shoulder in exasperation and by late that afternoon Fontana had the packers loaded plus the new rifles he'd especially wanted for Dull Knife.

"I sure wish you'd reconsider and stick around for a while." The proprietor stood looking up at Kyle as he settled in the saddle. "You're passing up the best deal you'll ever get anyplace in this country, and there's a couple of other things I'd like to ask you about too."

"No time for that now. We're going to get moving."

"Well can't you at least tell me if you're coming back? I mean it would be nice to know if I can depend on you to return with more pelts like these, sometime?"

"Like I said before, don't depend on anything. I don't make plans like that anymore. I might come back before winter and I might not."

Brady pulled at his chin in exasperation and stepped back as the buckskin-clad man reined the Appaloosa around and started down the alley.

"Remember what I said." He called after him. "You can trade for anything I've got here, goods you won't find within two hundred miles of here, and all first-class stuff too. Think about it Fontana, you're passing up one hell of an opportunity!"

But the pair kept on riding until they reached the street and turned out of sight, as he cussed under his breath then called his two pals over.

"Listen here, you two. Get saddled up and get yourself a packer too. I want you to follow him and find out exactly where he's headed. If he don't want to cooperate then we'll do it the hard way, but I want to know where he came from, and where he got all those pelts. He can't move very fast with those goods and that woman, so just stay back far enough that he don't know you're on him. Now get going."

"Dont'cha think that might be kind'a risky?" Buck cocked his head. "What if he heads up into Indian country, then what? I ain't gettin' myself scalped even for a ton of beaver, and I don't think Zinky here much wants to either."

"Stop your bellyachin' and use your head for something besides a hat rack. All this fur is double grade A prime. There's a fortune up there someplace and I'm not going to let it just slip through my fingers because that squaw man don't want to make a deal. I'll make my own deal once I find out where he's trapping, and you two will see some real money out of it too. Four or five days is probably all you'll need to see where he's headed, then swing around and get back here. Now, get hopping!"

As Kyle and Quiet Moon rode up into the first timber he stopped for a minute looking back down at the tiny community wondering about Brady.

"I think we'll keep on riding after dark for a while just in case one of our "friends" decides to try and follow us. I wouldn't put much past any of them. Did you see Brady's eyes when he saw the pelts? And you caused quite a stir yourself. I didn't want to tell you down there, but Buck and Zinky wanted to know if I'd consider selling you to them?" He smiled for a moment waiting to see what her reaction would be.

"Sell me? Is that what white men do, sell their woman like horses and guns? How much do you think I would bring, Kyle?"

Her face remained devoid of emotion and he immediately knew his little joke had not only fallen on deaf ears, but backfired too.

"I didn't mean it . . . that way." He tried retreating. "You know . . . I'd never consider doing anything like that. I just thought it was funny, that's all. I could never really "sell" anyone for any reason, and least of all you. You know how I feel, don't you?"

"Your face is turning red, Ky-le. Do you wish to tell me more about how you feel?"

"Well no, not right now. Listen, why don't we just drop the subject. I didn't mean anything by it anyway, let's just forget about it."

He pulled Snow Ball around, relieved to end the sticky conversation and did not see the trace of a satisfied smile flash across her face at besting him.

They rode past sundown and into the night giving the horses their head, then finally stopped and slept briefly before starting out again by first light. By noon they were zig zagging up the steep rock face of a huge stone mountain and when they reached its timbered plateau they stopped to rest the horses and Kyle dismounted, edging back toward the cliffy drop off, eyes narrowing as he knelt to study the panorama of shiny gray granite, dark timber pockets, and far to the south the misty green of rolling valleys where tiny Riverton sat.

For a long time he did not move—then just as he started to get to his feet he thought he saw something move so far below that he had to squint and cup both hands to his eyes concentrating hard trying to make it out. Was it elk, or moose on the move, or something far more dangerous, something he'd been thinking about ever since they'd left Brady's?

"Quiet Moon. Remember that brass tube I bought back in town, the one with glass in both ends? It's in my saddle bags, would you bring it to me, please?"

In a moment she was at his side as he pulled the telescope extensions out and put it to his eye, talking almost at a whisper.

"I bought this for Dull Knife . . . he's never seen a looking glass before, but now it might come in real handy."

Slowly the distant images cleared as he stayed on the glass several moments longer, then lowered it, turning to the woman.

"That's what I thought might happen. There's three horses down there following us, two riders and a packer. From now on we're going to have to be a lot more careful about our tracks. They're stilll a good half day behind us, but let's get going and make as much time as possible."

Moving fast across the plateau Kyle stayed to rocky ground and when they reached a rushing creek on the far side he turned the horses into it, splashing ahead for another mile until climbing out up a bare rock gully that led into thick timber. They rode steadily the rest of the day, climbing as they went, then stopped again after dark for a few hours rest, though he did not sleep and spent most of the time prowling restlessly.

Finally, near dawn he stopped pacing and sat down next to Quiet Moon watching her sleep, her rhythmic breathing soft and steady as he studied her long, black hair, the beautiful line of her face, wishing he didn't have to wake her to go. He knew how his love for her had grown over the months even though he'd never actually been able to tell her so out loud. Now, all he wanted was to get them safely back to the village and lose the riders following them as he'd promised Dull Knife he would. If those men following them did actually catch up somehow, would he really be able to kill them as he'd once promised the chief when asked? He'd lived with the Utes long enough now to know that life and death were nearly daily occurrences and those that cherished life had to be ready to take it at a moment's notice to survive themselves. Maybe, he thought, he was becoming more Indian than white man even in his thinking. Then he carefully roused Quiet Moon and they departed.

It took Buck and Zinky a full half day to top out on the plateau and when they did they suddenly ran out of tracks, casting about trying to pick them up again.

"Where in hell you figure they went?" Buck pushed back his sweat stained hat, shaggy black hair falling down to his shoulders as he rubbed tired eyes.

"I dunno', but all of a sudden it looks like maybe they figured out we was followin' them. You think they could'a seen us?"

Buck shook his head slowly twisting in the saddle looking around.

"Well, why don't we get ourselves across this plateau and see if we can't pick up tracks on the other side. There sure ain't nothin' to go on here."

Later when they reached the creek, following its gravelly berm with the same result, Buck finally pulled his horse to a stop and got down wearily.

"You know what? It'll be dark in another hour or two so why don't we just camp right here for the night? We can start out again in the morning. It don't make no sense to keep followin' somethin' we can't even see, does it? Beside, these horses could use a rest too."

"What about a fire?" Zinky piled off his mount.

"I don't think it'll hurt none if we keep it small. Besides, up this high it'll probably get pretty cold at night. Why don't you rustle us up some wood while I unsaddle the horses."

That night the worn out pair commiserated around a fire about their predicament, being sent out on a wild goose chase by Brady while he stayed in town warm and comfortable. The next morning when Buck awoke, shivering under a thin wool blanket, he pulled on cold boots and started for the creek nearby to fetch some coffee water. As he knelt splashing a little of the icy liquid on his face then wiping it off with a shirt sleeve, something caught his eye just under the surface, something thumb sized that had a glow all its own even though the sun wasn't up yet. He put the coffee pot down, pulled up his sleeve, and plunged his hand under the surface. When he brought it back up, opening it he froze in disbelief, rubbing the huge nugget around in his hand so mesmerized that he couldn't even call out to Zinky. It was gold, pure gold, a nugget so big and smooth it looked as if it had been polished, and more gold than he'd ever seen in his entire life in one lump!

Finally, he came to his feet yelling at his partner, then running to his blanket, yanking the covers back as he babbled wildly and the groggy man slowly sat up rubbing his face, trying to make some sense of the sudden commotion.

"Look at it Zink! It's pure Double D gold, I

tell'ya, just look at it, and there must be a whole lot more up and down this little creek too! We're gonna be rich, so rich we'll be able to go anywhere and buy anything we want. I say the hell with Fontana, we've found ourselves the mother lode right here and I ain't gonna take another step further!"

The little man staggered upright peering at the heavy lump of gold just handed him, then up to Buck.

"Well... what if we do find more? I mean, what'll we tell Brady?"

"Tell Brady? Why should we tell him a damn thing! He didn't send us up here to look for no gold, did he? We was suppose to be trackin' Fontana, right? This gold ain't none of his business. When we get back we'll just tell him he put the slip on us and we couldn't stay with him. How about that?"

"Well yeah, I guess that sounds right. Maybe whenever we get back to Riverton we'll just tell him we quit, then come back up here and work as much color out as we can before winter sets in. We'll just keep our trap shut like you said, and maybe we will get rich... PARTNER!"

Chapter Four

Yellow Iron Fever

When they finally reached the village the first thing Dull Knife did was send out scouts to be sure they were not followed, even though Kyle had not told him yet about the men trying to track them. After being satisfied they were alone, he questioned Fontana about the trip to Riverton as the buckskin man pulled a brand new rifle out of a top pack and handed it to the surprised red man.

"With these, your braves can take more game and even stop the Cheyennes who already have some rifles of their own. They will give you the same power you've seen me use with mine."

The chief slowly turned the gleaming weapon over in his hands, eyes flashing, then lifted it to his shoulder.

"I brought six of these and enough powder and lead to teach you and your braves how to shoot. You must practice just as I do, then no one will be able to best you. You'll be stronger than ever."

"I did not want you to travel to the white man's village of sticks, but this smoke pole has much power as you say. I am glad now you brought them back to me, but I still believe the white men that saw you will want to know where you came from and try to find you."

Kyle hesitated a moment longer then decided to tell Dull Knife the entire story rather than hide a lie.

"Two men did try to follow us, but I lost them far back in the mountains. I am sure they have turned back by now or we would have seen them. Do not trouble yourself over it. I was careful not to leave any tracks."

But Buck and Zinky hadn't turned back and instead stayed camped on the creek and the fabulous gold strike they'd discovered, working hard each day to pan out as much color as they possibly could, even driven to using their frying pan for a washer. Then each evening around the campfire their eyes gleamed with greed as the day's efforts were carefully poured into a heavy leather pouch until it was nearly three quarters full by week's end.

"We're pretty near out of food and got about as much gold as I'd want to pack back to town and still keep it quiet," Buck announced that Sunday. "What do'ya say we head on back to Riverton and get those supplies we need, then ride back here and make a good camp until the snow flies."

"Well yeah, but we're gonna have to be pretty careful not to let on when we see Brady again. He'd skin us alive if he ever caught wind of what we've got right here."

"We'll just tell him we quit, that's all. We'll tell 'em we're moving on to someplace else, and we're tired of workin' for practically nothing. We'll even buy our goods from him so he thinks we're heading out for sure, then once we get outt'a town we'll turn and head back up here."

"How much you figure we got, anyway?"

"I ain't sure, it'll have to be scale weighed, but John Younger out at the edge of town got that little assay office and he can tell us for sure. What I do know is that we've got enough to buy anything we want, and I'll tell him to keep his mouth shut about it too so he don't go blabbin' all over the place. Now, let's break camp and get an early start."

When the pair rode into Riverton four days later, Brady was quick to usher them into his trading post then lock the door peppering them with questions about Kyle and the woman only to be told they'd lost them in the mountains.

"Lost 'em, what do you mean you lost them! How in hell could you lose a man and woman pulling two pack horses!" he screamed at the pair.

"The only thing I can figure is he must'a rode nearly all night and got way ahead of us, or maybe they found out we were trailin' them? Why hell, Brady, that white man's half Indian anyway, and he thinks like 'em too. Once he got on solid rock we couldn't stay with 'em, and neither could you. We tried to find 'em for nearly a week, and you can't ask a man to do much more than that, on top of the chance that Indians might sneak up on you while you're asleep and maybe take your scalp."

"By God, you two idiots can't do anything I tell you to without fouling it up! If I'd known you were that dumb I'da went up there myself. Maybe I just ought to find myself a couple of new men who can handle what I give them to do, huh?"

"Well, we want to talk to you about that too, you see me and Zinky here we're gonn'a... quit anyway. We decided to head off maybe south out into plains country and get out of these damn mountains for a while. All the snow and freezing cold and winters, well we've just about had enough of it. You know what I mean? Besides, we ain't makin' any money workin' for you, so we figure it's time to go."

They eyed the proprietor a moment longer as rage built up in him, then he exploded again.

"You two ain't quitting nothing, understand! You idiots cost me something I wanted and I'm not going to just let you go blab your mouth off about the furs Fontana brought down here and start a rush by every peckerwood with a dozen traps and a mule. I let you in on this deal and now your gonn'a stay in until it's finished. You'll quit when I tell you you can quit and not a minute sooner, even if we have to haul my own traps back up there and find the area he worked ourselves. Now, get out of here before I take a bull whip to you and be sure you don't forget we're all in this together and I'm running the show. I'll call you back when I'm ready."

When they arrived at Buck's cabin they broke out a bottle and sat down trying to decide what to do next. After downing a couple of glasses and fortifying their backbone, Buck started thinking out loud.

"Maybe we just outt'a kill 'im straight out? Get 'im out of town someplace and let 'im have it where no one can find him?"

Zinky stared at his partner wide eyed then poured himself another drink, the fiery liquid burning its way down as he digested Buck's words.

"Well . . . why don't we try and find another way, at least not someplace anywheres around here. We might get found out?"

"Like what?"

"Ohhhh, I don't know, but I know I don't want no hangin' over my head, so we'd haf'ta get way out . . . like back up where we were. No one would find anyone up there, and especially not with winter comin' on. Maybe we could actually tell Brady about the gold?"

"You crazy!"

"No, not likely, because once he found out he'd forget all about them furs and want us to take him there. Probably try and cut us out of any deal if he had half the chance, but we'd beat him to it, finish him off back there. I'm tired of takin' his guff anyway and have been for a long time. I say let's tell 'im and see what happens. If he goes for it like I think he will, we'll know what to do once we get 'im up there."

Buck's eyes glazed over momentarily as he admired his partner's guile. Every once in a while old Zinky actually came up with a pretty good idea, but this topped them all, a grim smile wrinkling his face as he stuck out a stubby hand.

"Nice goin' partner. Tomorrow we'll set the trap!"

When they told Brady the whole story the next morning his anger was overwashed by the fantastic story of golden wealth, and when they poured the nuggets and gold dust out on the counter, his eyes narrowed with greed as his mind raced, then he walked quickly to lock the front door and pull down window shades.

"All right, you two. You just got yourself a third partner, but I'm still calling the shots. I'll have to stand for all the supplies we'll need to take with us, and I'll get old man Finny to watch the store while we're gone and we'll have to move quick before winter really sets in for good. Because I'm going to have to furnish everything, and because you both lied through your teeth to me, I'm taking a full half share of anything we find. You two can split what's left, and I ain't asking you whether you like it or not. Now, let's start getting everything together. We should be able to pull out of here in two days if we hustle."

When the threesome rode out of town past the last log buildings and up into timber they were pulling two heavily loaded pack horses. Over the next four days they climbed farther back, each man's mind fixed on the fortune that awaited them but only two knowing there would never be a three-way split.

On the fifth day they reached the creek and quickly set up a permanent camp with tent and supplies stacked close by. Then they hurriedly grabbed up gold pans and immediately began working the shallows right in front of camp. Brady trembled as he sloughed off the last bit of black sand in the rim of the pan to see the wide crescent of small nuggets and golden flakes nestled there. The next day vanished quickly into two, three, then a week of steady work with pouches beginning to bulge. Each night around the campfire he would fill the tin used as a measuring cup right to the top then pour off his half, giving Buck and Zinky the rest to split between themselves as both of them watched with smoldering resentment but biding their time.

One evening into the second week they'd finished eating then divided up the goods as usual, when Brady knelt by the fire to light his cigar with a flaming stick. All that day Buck and Zinky had been eyeing each other with knowing glances, and now quietly Buck rose to his feet and grabbed a shovel next to the tent, bringing it up over his head with both arms, then swung it down with a shattering smash that sent Brady face first into the fire as he writhed and screamed trying to roll out of the consuming flames, only to be hit again and again until Zinky grabbed him by the legs and dragged him clear so Buck could finish off the job.

Finally done with their fiendish work both men stood gasping, the stench of burning flesh strong in their nostrils.

"Let's drag him downhill and bury him!" Buck fought to catch his breath.

"Why bury him? Let's just get 'im far enough away from here that the wolves will finish him off. That won't take long soon as they find him."

Then they tied a rope around the dead man's legs and dragged him off into the night.

The pair stayed on Nugget Creek for another two weeks working feverishly each day to amass as much gold as possible. Then when pickings began to thin they moved camp farther upstream and topped off their "bank" in another ten days of work until the first hard freeze licked icy tongues at pools and backwater eddies with a skim of ice, and they decided it was time to pull out.

"What'll we say about Brady when we get back to town?" Zinky questioned.

"We'll just tell 'em the Indians killed him and we had to run for our lives to keep from gettin' the same medicine. There ain't gonna be enough left of him to find anyway. Now, let's get these packers loaded and make tracks outta here."

The long, cold ride down out of the high country was tempered by the heavy leather bags full of gold that both men carried and each evening when they made camp they would pull them out again, pouring the contents out on a blanket assuring themselves they were as rich as they thought. When they finally did ride back into Riverton, several men on the street ran up alongside them asking questions, and when they arrived at the store and collapsed in chairs the crowd grew even larger as both men poured down several quick shots of whiskey until Buck got up waving his hand for quiet.

"Brady's dead! The Utes got 'im and they'da got me and Zink too if we hadn't run for our lives. Right now our scalps could'a been dangling from some buck's lodge pole."

The men erupted in a blizzard of shouted questions, all astonished at their daring escape from certain death until one brought up the question of the store itself.

"What's going to happen to the trading post here? It's the only thing we got for goods from the outside. What if the Indians decide to come all the way down here and make war on us too?"

The pair looked at each other for a moment, then Buck had a sudden brainstorm.

"Now, listen here. First of all them Utes ain't gonna come down here. They only get in a killin' mood when whites head up into their country. Second, Brady didn't have no kin as far as I know, but me and Zinky here well, we was sort'a like brothers to him. We could maybe buy the store and keep it runnin' for a while until someone comes in from outside and buys it up, or just take it over like it was willed to us. I know for sure the Brady would'a wanted it that way, don't you Zink?"

His partner was so dumbstruck for a moment that he couldn't answer, then snapped out of it shaking his head vigorously yes until he found his voice.

"Why sure, that's what Frank would'a wanted alright. We'll try and make a go of it at least for now until we decide what we want to do. We was fixin' to pack up and move east, but just to help the rest of you boys we might stick around for a while longer."

A ripple of applause then shouts of support coursed through the crowd as both murderers stood and accepted congratulations.

And so the pair settled in managing the trading post and taking anything they wanted for themselves until supplies finally began running low and Buck sent Zinky on the long wagon ride south to Casper to find their supplier, the Lindstrom Freight Company, with enough gold to pay the bill.

"We'll settle up for the rest when your wagon makes it up to Riverton." Zinky opened the pouch pouring the golden nuggets on the counter asking for a scale to be sure he didn't pay anymore than necessary.

"It's hard to believe old Brady is dead." Strom Lindstrom shook his head, eyeing the little man carefully. "You say the Indians got him?"

"That's the truth of it, alright, and they damn near got me and my partner too, but we outrun 'em."

"Brady never paid me in gold before, always either cash or sometimes when he had them, furs. Where did you boys come on all this color?"

For a moment Zinky almost panicked as he tried to come up with something that sounded plausible, clearing his throat stalling for time.

"Well . . . we just do a little pannin' from time to time up there. There ain't much really, but we gathered this up over a couple of years, and now that we're runnin' the post we just decided to spend some of it. There's nothing steady you could make any kind of a livin' at, that's for sure! Now, how long did you say it would be before you get your wagon up there?"

"If we don't get no snow maybe eight or nine days. If it hits, two weeks. Brady's dead, huh? I'd never thought he'd go out like that, not by Indians anyway."

"Yeah, well you never know what's gonna happen now do'ya. Be sure and get them supplies started north as soon as possible."

Zinky wasn't out the door five minutes when Strom headed for the loading dock looking for his brother Carl. He led him into a back room looking around quickly to be sure they were alone, pouring out the nuggets.

"Look'it this. Some character was just in here who says he took over Brady's up in Riverton and used this for a down payment on a delivery. Says he and his partner just scratched it up, but that doesn't make any sense to me, and he says Brady was killed by Indians, but you and I know Brady was about the last man to leave town and head up into Indian country. Nothing in his whole story adds up except this gold. It's real enough and I'd sure like to know where he got it, wouldn't you?"

That evening both Lindstroms decided to freight the supplies themselves and try to find out exactly what was going on. If there really was a gold strike they wanted to be in on it, and just to keep the information all in the family they also told their two grown sons Darrel and John, and their uncle Del. That way they'd have their own family group together for whatever might come. But Strom made the mistake of locking the nuggets away in the store safe and the next morning when the bookkeeper, Jolene Betters, opened the safe for business she found the heavy leather pouch curiously opening it, remembering it wasn't there when she locked up the previous evening. After a startled look inside she quickly put it back but that evening when she returned home she told her husband about it and before the week was out the word of a possible gold strike somewhere near Riverton was out.

By the time the Lindstroms big freighter pulled out three dozen excited men were already on the road north with more coming, and when they did reach town all asking the same questions, Buck and Zinky knew their secret was out, though they continued to deny knowing anything about it and argued heatedly between themselves about what to do about it.

Undeterred, the gold seekers spread out panning any piece of water they could find, regardless of how small, then started moving up into the foothills around town when nothing was found. Finally, the pair decided there was nothing left to do but close up the store and head back to Nugget Creek to stake a legal claim before the growing hoard searched far enough into the back country that someone might actually stumble on the golden placers.

Then, the first snows of winter began to lace the high country and when Buck and Zinky arrived they quickly threw up a small, roughly built one room log cabin so they could stick it out as long as possible. But in less than two weeks the first party of men trailing them found the little waterway and began doing their own panning. The pair tried to stay to themselves as much as possible, but one evening as another light snow began to fall three men who were camped downstream came into their camp just as Buck was stoking a fire. The leader wore a heavy, full length buffalo coat and wide brimmed hat and looked at them for a moment before introducing himself.

"My name's Bard Cutter, and these two men here are my partners, Jim Seamis and Carl Latrobe."

"What d'ya want?" Buck snapped, unhappy to have another bunch of strangers come barging into their place, sizing them up cautiously.

"We don't want anything, but Carl here was working up a side canyon yesterday when he found this. I thought we ought to show it to somebody else around here, and you fellas seem to know the lay of the land."

Cutter opened his coat flap and pulled out a rag wrapped around what looked like the tattered cloth of a pants leg and in it a piece of leg bone.

"The animals have chewed it up pretty bad, but you can see what it is alright, and there's more bones where he found this. I don't know who the poor devil was, but when this snow finally drives us out we're going to try looking up some kind of law and turn it over to them. There may be someone looking for whoever this was, or what's left of him."

The pair stared at the men without saying anything for a moment dumbstruck with fear. Then Buck tried to stammer an answer.

"Why hell . . . whoever that was has probably been dead for years. Ain't nobody gonna be lookin' for him now. It could'a been just about any drifter wandering through here, huh Zink?"

The little man nodded his head quickly but did not speak.

"If I was you, I'd just bury whatever's left and let it go at that. Indians, maybe a mountain panther or grizzly bear probably got 'im. There's no tellin' what. Why worry about it anyway? Just giv 'im a Christian burial and forget about it."

"I don't think we'll do that. I heard someone say back in Riverton that the man who owned the trading post, what's his name?"

"You mean Brady?" Latrobe volunteered.

"Yeah, that's it. Anyway I heard this Brady was lost someplace up in this country. Maybe this is him?"

"That can't be! The Indians got Brady, and we know that for sure because we was with 'im when it happened. Me and my partner had to ride for our lives, but he didn't make it and once them Utes get their dirty hands on'ya any white man is gonna die a slow death, not be left layin' in some canyon. I'll bet poor ol' Brady's scalp is danglin' right now from some buck's lodge pole!"

"Well, maybe, but we'll just gather up what we can like I said and take it back anyway. It's a damn poor way for any man to die no matter who he was. We're not animals like the Utes. At least we can take care of our own. We're going to head back to camp now. I just wanted someone else to know about it."

When the men left Buck and Zinky drew closer around the fire talking low and fast trying to warm their hands.

"Dammit, I told'ya we should'a buried him!" Buck hissed. "Now his damn ghost is trying to come back and haunt us, and if those three go ahead and do what they just said, we might be in some big trouble."

"We ain't got time to worry about that now. What we'd better do is think about our own necks. We've got some pretty good color so maybe we just ought to clear outta here while we can? By the time those three get back down to where there's any law we can be a helluva long ways from here. Why take any chances we don't have to? Maybe we could head west where no one knows us, and we could live pretty good for a long time on what we've got plus what's back at the store. What d'ya say to it, Buck? I don't want to be no party to a hangin', especially if the ropes got my name on it."

By mid-morning the next day they'd broken camp and had the packers loaded leaving everything behind they didn't need to reach Riverton. Then Buck walked down to the creek one last time mumbling to himself.

"Of all the damn dumb fool luck this has to be it. Just when we finally hit it big we've got to clear out and leave a fortune over a bag of bones and some scraps of cloth."

"Buck, let's get goin'!" Zinky called from the saddle, and finally he stooped down picking up a handful of gravel tossing it across the water in disgust. Then he turned and headed back to his horse.

They traveled light and fast winding their way down out of the snowy mountains until they reached town, then stayed only long enough to resupply themselves and change horses. Buck opened the store safe and pulled out the leather pouches of gold, then that very same night they saddled up and rode out of town past the last log buildings heading someplace even they weren't sure of.

But back up in the high country on Nugget Creek, Bard and his partners still took the time to continue searching the area where Latrobe had found the first remains, and two days later they turned up something that gave them further answers to the identity of the unknown victim.

"Hey, look'it here!" Seamis called to his friends, sweeping away the light covering of snow and leaves from a shiny gold chain then pulling up a mud encrusted watch as he rubbed it clean with his thumb.

"It's got an inscription on it . . . says, to Frank Brady from his brother . . . Ike."

Bard came running up to examine the timepiece for himself.

"Them two up the creek said Brady was killed by Utes, but no Indian would have left a gold watch like this just laying on the ground. There's something fishy about both of them that I didn't like from the start. Let's head up there and show them what we've got and see what they have to say about it, and keep your pistols handy just in case they try to pull something."

But when they reached the camp and found it abandoned plus the goods left behind, they were more sure than ever that the two knew far more than they were telling.

"They lit out of here in a big hurry." Bard pushed his hat back on his head pursing his lips and thinking out loud. "I think one of us should ride down to Casper and tell the law what we've found up here. What do you say?"

But neither man volunteered and just looked at each other shrugging slightly.

"We can't just let those two ride away and say nothing, can we?"

Latrobe took off his hat and ran his hands through matted hair, then looked up at Bard.

"Listen. Winter's right around the corner and when it hits none of us are going to be able to stay. Why don't we pan out as much color as we can then head down to Casper together. What will it be, another two weeks, maybe three? Why run for it now? Those two are already probably fifty miles away from here."

"That's just the point." Bard countered. "The longer we wait the farther away they'll get until no one will ever find them."

But his partners were not moved and just stood silently looking at each other.

"All right then, I'll go. I'll do it myself, and you two stay here and take care of the diggings. Once I reach Casper there's no sense coming all the way back up here, so I'll just wait until you come down, then we'll split up the goods. Is that alright?" And the three agreed.

The next morning Bard left his partners and started down stream running into the Lindstroms camped a quarter mile away, stopping long enough to tell them what they'd found and where he was going. Strom slowly took the pipe from his mouth thunderstruck by the news of a possible murder, and the pair involved in it.

"You sure it's Brady's watch?" he asked as his brother and the boys came up.

"Sure enough. Here, see for yourself." He pulled it out and handed it down as Strom turned it over slowly in his hands, shaking his head in amazement.

"Well, I'll tell you something. I didn't like the looks of that pip-squeak when he came into our store and I told brother Carl here the very same thing. That cock-and-bull story of his was about as wild sounding as he looked, except he did have some real color to pay for what he wanted. I knew there hadn't been a gold strike around Riverton in years, but yet he had some real goods. That's why we came up to see for ourselves. I didn't believe him then and I don't believe him now, but maybe I can help you out a little. I want my son Darrel here to head back to Casper with you and take what color we've got home along with a message to our family. You could probably use a little company yourself, couldn't you?"

"Yes, if you've got a mind to, I'll take him

along. What's the name of the sheriff back there?"

"It's John Darnel. He's a good man, but if those two left for parts unknown he's not going to chase them all over God's creation. He stays mostly just in the county. Family man you know, but he might be able to get hold of a federal marshal or even the U.S. cavalry if they happen through, though they're never on any kind of fixed schedule. You tell John we talked and I sent you down. It'll help because we're kin. I married one of his cousins, Darrel," he said to his son, "You tell mom we'll be up here until the snow flies for good and that won't be much more than another two or three weeks, and tell her not to worry and look after the business until we get back down. Now you go saddle a horse and get yourself some grub. You two be careful just in case that bunch up the creek is still around here someplace, and take a good rifle along with your pistol. Just sit easy mister, he'll have his stuff together in a few minutes, then you can head on out."

Twenty minutes later the pair started down the creek as Darrel twisted in the saddle and waved good-bye. Then they were swallowed up in snow-laced timber.

Chapter Five

The Warning

Now winter came in a flurry of heavy snows whipped by frigid winds and even the elk and deer were finally forced to start their long journeys down out of the high ranges, and with them Dull Knife and his tribe. They had to stay close to their winter meat supply and that meant lower country, but these moves always were accompanied by a great deal of trepidation for that would bring the red men closer to white settlements springing up along the foothills, and a chance encounter Kyle would have less than a week after they re-established camp.

    He was out with a hunting party eager to try their new rifles when suddenly they heard distant voices down canyon and crept to a drop off to see what it was. Far below they made out the tiny figures of two white men kneeling next to an ice-bound creek, and just back of them a rough hewn log lean-to nearly covered in new snow. By signing, the six hunters quietly made their way down until Fontana was close enough to ease out on a house-size boulder watching the pair intently as they swirled a pan full of dirt in the freezing water, instantly recognizing they were panning for gold. Just behind him, one of the warriors clicked the hammer on his rifle back to full cock, but he turned quickly shaking his head "no," putting a finger to his lips.

It was clear the men were excited as they talked gesturing back and forth and so engrossed in conversation that they did not notice Fontana as he stood slowly above them in plain sight, and finally spoke.

"What are you two doing here?"

The pair whirled, jumping to their feet dropping the pan and pulling pistols, wide eyed and half startled out of their wits.

"I wouldn't pull them off, not unless you want to die right where you stand. These braves behind me will fill you full of lead before you can get off two shots. Now put those six guns back where they belong. If we wanted to kill you it would already be over by now. Put 'em back."

Still stunned by their sudden appearance, Strom Lindstrom took a few tentative steps forward, squinting at the buckskin clad man in a fur cape that spoke like a white man but looked like an Indian.

"Who in hell are you, anyway?" He finally found his voice. "You white or Indian?"

"Hold your tongue and stop asking any questions. The only thing I want to know is what you two are doing up here. You're a long ways from home, aren't you?"

"What are we doing . . . we're panning for gold, what does it look like?"

"Gold? Do you know where you're at? You're on Ute ground and that's asking for more trouble than any gold is worth. You're lucky I found you before these warriors did, or they'd already have your hair by now. Take some good advice while you still can. Pack up your goods and get out of here while you've got the chance. You won't get another one!"

"Clear out of here? There's at least three dozen other men down this canyon doing the same thing. Do you think they're going to just pull and run for it because you and these Utes don't like them being here? Who are you anyway, what's your name, and why are you riding around with a bunch of savages?"

"My name's Fontana, and why I'm with these people is nobody's business but my own. I don't care if there's three dozen or thirty dozen down there. I'm telling you, you'd better make some sense to them or they'll never leave these mountains alive. You're not going to match the whole Ute nation, and that's what you'll be up against. A lot of men will die."

"Well, there's already been one man killed up here and there might be others but plenty of them will be redskins too, you ought to think about that while you're making all these threats. You actually live with these featherheads?"

"I do, and I know their mind. They won't tolerate any whites in this country, and as far as they're concerned you're trespassing on sacred ground. You said so yourself, someone's already been killed over a little bit of dust."

"Yeah, that was Brady from down at Riverton, and everyone said it was your friends here that killed him, but now me and a few others know better."

"Brady? You mean Brady that ran the trading post?"

"That's him alright, but how did you know who he was?"

"I did some trading with him at the end of summer. He had two men who worked for him, what was their name?"

"Buck Loon and Doad Zinky's the ones you're talking about. They're also the ones we figure killed Brady then tried to blame those redskins of yours. One of the miners found what was left of him and now my son and another man are riding for Casper to put the law on them."

"All that's your business so long as you don't bring them back up here. When you get back down canyon you'd better get those other men together and tell them what I said, then make them believe it. These Utes don't come down into your valleys and ranches, and they don't want you coming up here. I don't care if all the gold in the world is up in these mountains. None of it is worth your life or anyone else's, is it?"

"Are you telling me you don't want a pouch full of these nuggets? Is that what you expect me to believe, or do you just want us out of here so you've got it all to yourself? Why else would you be living like a squaw man if that wasn't it?"

"I'm tired of talking to you. You can believe what you want, but remember what I said. You don't leave here and there's going to be dead men scattered all over this canyon and you two will likely be some of them. Get those others out or they'll end up just like Brady. Take this warning for what it's worth, because there won't be a second one!"

Kyle turned and started back up through snowy timber, the braves right on his heels as the brothers watched them go. Then Strom yelled after him.

"Hey . . . you better tell your friends I can't just make everyone keep out of these mountains! Come spring they'll be back and probably a lot more of them once the word gets out that there's gold up here. You listening to me . . . I can't stop them and neither can you!"

Nearly out of sight above, Kyle stopped, staring back down.

"You'd better!" Then he turned and was gone.

When the hunting party reached the village he told Dull Knife about the encounter but the old man did not seem to be surprised as he took him aside, explaining he and his people knew about the golden pebbles all along.

"We do not pick it up because we cannot use it. You cannot eat it or make weapons from it. You cannot wear it in winter to keep warm. Only white men dig in the ground like squirrels to find it. Now that they know it is here there will be much trouble for it makes them mad. They have already scattered across much of the buffalo plains like the sheep they bring with them, and now they want to come up into our ancient land too. There will be a war. I see no way to stop it. We will not let them live here even if we have to kill every one of them."

Kyle thought for a moment before answering, trying to find a way around it all.

"For now, winter will send most of them back down, but come spring they will try to come back as you say. I told them not to, but I do not think they will listen. Now, can I speak for a moment about something else that is heavy on my heart?"

Dull Knife nodded, as Kyle took him by the arm and walked away where no one could hear him speak, then told him about his life before he came up into Ute country and what was once his family before they were murdered. He also explained that he'd not only found a new life with his people, but a new love in Quiet Moon that had only grown stronger since his arrival, and here, in winter camp, he wanted to marry her in the tribal custom if she would have him.

The red man looked Kyle straight in the face for a long time without answering, then slowly put his hand on his shoulder.

"You have shown me you are not like other white men. Maybe the time has come to take another woman. Every man needs a woman to cook his food, to warm his bed, and bear him sons to carry his name. The day may come when even the Great Spirit speaks to you, though no other white man has ever heard his voice. Take this woman now while the land sleeps because when the warm sun rises again there will be little time for it."

In the Ute way Quiet Moon stayed in her lodge for three days without seeing Kyle or anyone else, fasting and purifying herself. On the fourth she accepted the presence of three women who dressed her in the finest buckskin and winter furs and tied the teepee flap open to show she opened her heart to Kyle as his woman and wife. Then the chief took him there representing his request and also asked for the union, giving it his blessing. The women exited the lodge and finally Quiet Moon came out and walked up to Kyle, taking his hand in hers and speaking only in her native tongue, as Dull Knife stepped back toward the ring of men and women watching the solemn ceremony.

"I will be your wife as you ask, but are you sure this is what you want for both of us? Do you believe a Ute woman and a white man can live as one? I know there will be people among both yours and mine that scorn such a thing. It will not be an easy thing, Kyle."

He stepped forward taking both her hands in his then leaned down and kissed her lightly on the forehead, to the astonishment of most women there who had never seen such a strange thing before.

"I ask you only this. Do you love me as you know I do you?"

"Yes, I have felt the same thing between us."

"Then neither you or I should care what other people think because if we let that happen we will always be afraid of someone else's thoughts, and not let our love rule our lives. Nothing else matters to me. Just you and I, and what we feel for each other."

She stepped back slowly, pulling him with her until reaching the lodge entrance.

"Then come into your home and that of your wife, for she awaits you with all the joy her heart can hold."

He stopped just outside and turned to look briefly at the people standing in the snow without murmuring a word, but that was the Ute way. There was no cheering, no back slapping, no wild celebration, but Kyle Fontana was supremely happy. Then he stepped inside pulling the flap shut behind him.

Quiet Moon stood only a few steps away

and he went to her, folding his arms around her then kissing her gently full on the lips for only the second time, briefly, then pulled back as she looked up at him.

"Why do you close your eyes? Do you not like what you see?"

"Of course I do." He was caught by surprise, struggling to find an answer that would make sense. "It's just that . . . well, I close my eyes because . . . it makes me feel better, that's the only way I can explain it . . ."

Before he could finish she pulled his head down close and experimented with the strange sensation again in her own way, holding him there longer until finally pulling back but just slightly.

"Is this the white man's way of making love?"

"Yes, part of it. It's been a long time since I had a woman in my arms, something I thought I might never do again until I found you."

"Then we must be meant for each other, Kyle, because I have never had any feelings for a man until you came here."

She tried the kiss again, but this time he lifted her completely off the ground and walked a few steps until lowering both of them on thick fur robes and began kissing her neck, throat, then further down. Suddenly the gold, the miners, the trouble that it all portended didn't mean anything anymore. They were man and wife there next to the flickering fire and their unbridled desire matched the dancing tongues of flames.

Winter was brutal even at these lower elevations, but it was a winter of joy and love like Kyle had never known, even though in the back of his mind there was that gnawing fear the coming spring would be like no other, not only for him and his wife, but all the Ute people. He hunted sometimes with other red men, schooling them in their rifle shooting as they became more proficient, and sometimes just he and Quiet Moon would go out for two or three days. On one of his hunts he took her back above Nugget Creek to peer down at the little waterway now frozen solid and covered in snow. It was quiet, peaceful, only a sleeping child of the great mountains in which it flowed as it was meant to be, and sitting there in the saddle he wished winter would never end.

But slowly, inexorably, it began to wane and with it Dull Knife mobilized his warriors to return to the golden waterway for the return of white men he was sure would come, instructing Kyle to be their leader.

"You once lived as they do," he told him solemnly. "Talk to them in their own tongue one more time. Tell them if they try to stay, there will be war and many will die. Once you said you would fight your own people if there was no other way. Now, I believe that time has come. Go and keep them out Kyle. There will be no more talk."

After returning to the creek, they camped on a high rim above it and Kyle stationed scouts each day along a broad front where they could look over the country below still laced in melting snows, and the few routes that led in. Near the beginning of the second week one of the red men sent a runner to him to come quick, and he did so taking the "looking glass" he'd given the chief earlier as a gift. When he arrived, the scout pointed far below to a tiny line of riders winding their way up the partially frozen creek and Kyle focused it carefully until the images became clear.

They were white men all right, but what caught his eye most was their dress, for all seemed to be wearing the same dark color uniforms in blue. Then it dawned on him; they must be U.S. Cavalry horsemen alerted by the miners who left last fall. Now they'd sent for protection and gotten it, as he watched them finally stop at one log lean-to and begin to unload the string of pack mules they'd brought in.

Finally, he stood issuing orders for the warriors to remain there while he rode down to confront this new and more powerful threat, and one far more grave than just the few dozen miners he'd expected all along. Several braves protested his decision to go alone but he reminded them that Dull Knife had placed him in charge, then mounted Snow Ball and started the long circuitous route down.

Later, as he approached the busy camp one of the soldiers finally saw him only after he closed to within fifty yards, shouting an alarm and running for his rifle.

"Captain Cutter, come quick. There's an Indian here!"

In a moment, the young officer was up front with the rest of the troops at his back as he stepped forward and studied this strange looking red man in front of him.

"Do you speak American?" he called out, lifting a hand in greeting while his other rested on the leather pistol holster at his side.

Kyle pulled his horse to a stop but did not answer or step down for a moment longer as he studied the camp, its supplies, and the number of men there, then finally back to Cutter.

"Yes, I speak American, in fact I was probably speaking it before you were born."

The captain's jaw literally dropped in amazement before he quickly recovered his composure and stepped closer looking up at Fontana, eyes narrowing.

"For God's sake you look like a white man! Are you?"

"I am." Kyle nodded. "What are you and your men doing in this country? You're on Ute ground, don't you know that?"

"Ute ground? Since when do the Utes own this or any other place? This is about to become a territory of the United States government, and some day it might even become a state."

"Since when? Since long before either you or I or our mothers or fathers ever set foot on this continent, that's when. Their people have lived here so long even they don't know for sure when their ancestors first came here and there were no white men when they did, I can tell you that for sure. In fact they rarely even saw whites until they found a little color last year in this creek you're standing next to. That's why you're here, isn't it?"

"What in hell kind of a white man are you anyway, talking like that and taking their side? You're even dressed like one of them. What happened to you, did you lose your mind or something? What's your name, I mean your real name, and not something they gave you?"

"My name is Kyle Fontana, but it won't mean anything to you or anyone else. Besides, it's not important. What is, is that you're smart enough to listen to me and understand what I'm telling you before you start an Indian war you and everyone else in this part of the country will regret."

"Wait a minute! I'm here on explicit orders from General Whitehead to protect the miners that will be up here in another week or so, and I mean to carry those orders out to the fullest, Mr. Fontana, if that's what you want me to call you."

"You do and you'll carry out a death sentence you'll never live down. The Utes are not going to let you or anyone else come back in here whether you've got "orders," or not. I came here to speak on behalf of Dull Knife, the chief of the Ute nation, and you'd better listen. Take these men and leave while you still can. Don't argue about it, and don't get your back up, just do it."

Cutter's eyes drifted off Fontana up along the snowy rim above, then finally back to him.

"You here alone?"

"No, I'm not. I came here to give the message I just did. Go back to your general and tell him he's making a big mistake if he thinks he can send you or anyone else up here and just take over. That's not going to happen. They'll send the whole Ute nation down on you. You're in their country now, not yours."

The officer studied Fontana even more now without a quick answer, wondering about him personally.

"Let me ask you something, Fontana. How did you end up like this?" He pointed to his buckskin dress and furs. "What happened to you that you'd rather stay with Indians than your own people? It must have been pretty bad, to make you go against your own kind."

"I stay because I choose to, and besides, you couldn't understand even if I told you, which I won't. Just take what I've told you and believe it. The Utes have never asked for a war with whites but they'll give you one if you push for it, and that's exactly what you're doing coming up here."

"Well, you can tell this . . . Dull Knife, that the United States government is going to come looking for him to sign a land treaty and not just here but all along the northern front. Many of the southern tribes have already done so, and are being treated perfectly well. If you really want to help him and his people you'll convince him that's the best way to maintain peace, whether they understand it right now or not. Eventually, they'll realize we were right."

"No, no they won't, because I won't sell them out like that. Without these lands these people will die. It's their heart, soul, and religion. It's the only thing they've ever known, and the only thing that means anything to them. You can't haul them off to some reservations someplace like caged animals and expect them to live through it, and I won't help you try. Remember what I've just said. Get you and your men out of here, and tell this General Whitehead of yours to stay out."

"I won't be threatened by the likes of you, sir. In fact, I'm ordering you down off that horse. I'm sure the general will find you most interesting. Now get off!"

"Not likely!" Kyle whipped Snow Ball around kicking him away under pounding hooves as they flew for the safety of timber, and shouts then shots rang out behind them, bullets whining and cracking off branches as the pines swallowed them up and he urged the big horse higher for the safety of the rim.

Cutter ran for his horse, shouting orders for half his men to stay and guard camp while the rest mounted up and thundered after Fontana. Red Star, second in command, witnessed the wild scene below and ordered the warriors to prepare to shoot the moment Kyle neared the top, Snow Ball lunging higher and higher under his master's short whip.

Finally the big Appaloosa sped just under the rim and a ragged volley of shots rent the icy air like bogus thunder, instantly bringing down the captain's horse in the lead and sending him flying head over heels over the falling animal, while two more blue coats behind him spun from their saddles hit by hot lead. Now, chaos reined as the horse soldiers in the rear tried to frantically pull their mounts around out of the line of deadly fire, and Cutter crawled from the snowbank he'd landed in, scrambling back down the trail afoot dodging more bullets.

The instant Kyle dismounted he ran for the Utes lining the rim and ordered them to hold their fire, watching the mass confusion below as the cavalrymen retreated until finally out of rifle range, and Red Star came to his side.

"The white soldiers did not listen to your words."

"No, not yet, but maybe after this they will."

"I do not think so. They tried to kill you and you share the same skin. Dull Knife must council for war or there will be more of them next time." But Kyle did not answer.

Over the next four days Captain Cutter tried to lead his men over the top through several other routes but the red men repelled them each and every time. Then, on the fifth, they began to break camp as Kyle watched intently through the "looking glass" telescope while several warriors gathered around him.

"They're leaving." He spoke in their own tongue. "Maybe they've had enough. Red Star, I'll stay here another two days to be sure they've gone, but I want you to ride for the village and tell Dull Knife what has happened here. Tell him I'll return in eight suns, and I've got one more job to do first. Go now."

The warrior and half the braves had been gone for less than an hour when Fontana saw a single rider slowly winding his way back up the trail carrying a white flag of truce on a stick.

"Don't fire," he ordered the red men around him, watching him climb higher until finally he was within shouting distance.

"Fontana . . . come down. I want to talk to you. Fontana, can you hear me?"

Instantly he recognized Captain Cutter's voice and stood, pulling Snow Ball over then swinging atop him, ordering his braves to keep an eye on everything below and fire a warning shot in case this was some kind of a trap. Then he urged the spotted horse over the top and carefully down the winding trail until stopping a few yards away from the young officer.

"I've lost five men and I'm pulling my troops out for now, but I'll be back with a regiment if that's what it takes. I want you to know you're responsible for their deaths, and that makes you guilty of murder. I don't care how you dress, or what you call yourself, you're still a white man subject to white man's law!"

"You rode all the way up here to tell me that? Because if you did you're a fool. YOU lost those men with your own stupidity after I warned you to leave here. When you get back to wherever it is you're going, you can tell this General Whitehead of yours that the Utes aren't the plains' people he's been subjugating, and if he comes back up here either with or without you, he's going to regret it even more than you do now. Take your dead men and go, Cutter, and remember what I've said."

"I'm not done with you yet! I came up for one more reason and you'd better listen to it. I'll give you one last chance to turn yourself over to me right now and come back to face these charges. If you do so, I'll try to see to it that you're not hung, and I want to know the location of the Ute village too. If you refuse, it's just a matter of time before you're run down and shot like any other renegade Indian. Just because you've won this skirmish, don't think you can beat the whole United States Cavalry, because you can't. If you have any sense left in you you'll take advantage of what I'm offering, or mark yourself for a hangman's rope. Now, what's it going to be?"

"Turn your horse around and ride out of here, and don't talk to me about white man's law or justice. I've seen it in action before and I've had a belly full of it. It's as crooked as that stick you've got in your hand. Get out of here Cutter, and keep on going. Don't come back."

The captain stared at his nemesis with rage and indignation only a moment longer, then finished with one final warning.

"You've just put a noose around your neck, and when they do it I'll be there to watch you drop. We'll hunt you down wherever you go, no matter how long it takes!"

"I said get going, and tell your general to stay out of these mountains, or the Utes will bury him up here too."

Chapter Six

General Stanton Terrell Whitehead

Captain John Cutter stood at attention in General Whitehead's office, his clothes and boots splattered with mud from the battle and long ride south to the military post, as the portly senior officer listened to his report in stony silence puffing slowly on a strong, cheroot cigar. When he'd finished, Whitehead lifted himself out of the squeaky chair. Pursing his lips in thought, he came around the desk and over to a large map hanging on the wall, running a stubby finger up its surface.

"You say you encountered this man, this Fontana and the Utes someplace up here?" He turned with raised eyebrow, as Cutter came forward studying it for a moment then nodded.

"Yes sir, that looks pretty close."

"And you say, he was actually leading these Indians like some kind of chief, is that right? They took orders directly from him?"

"They did, sir."

"And how many of these red men did he have against you when you tried to capture him?"

For a moment the answer stuck in Cutter's throat as he took a deep breath grimacing slightly.

"I'm . . . not sure sir."

"You mean to tell me you don't know? What kind of officer would go up against a force of hostiles without knowing what he was facing? You lost how many men, captain?"

"Five, sir."

"And all of them trying to take one individual dressed like a wild man?"

"They had the high ground on us and were in cover. I didn't have the time to make a count, my only thought was to try and bring him back here to you for whatever disposition you saw fit. Once the fighting started I was only trying to save my men, but I know it was a large force."

The general shook his head, walked back to his desk, and sat down.

"Didn't you learn anything back east in the academy? You broke a number of basic rules with your unfounded actions and now you've given those savages a victory they don't deserve, while also making them bolder because of it. From what you've told me they had every advantage on you and you led your men right into the face of their fire. What did you expect, that they'd all drop their rifles and give up?"

"I was only trying to carry out orders, sir . . . I guess I didn't expect to run into anything like that, and especially not a white man leading Indians."

Whitehead pulled at his beard, slowly letting the anger dissipate, leaning back in the padded chair.

"It's obvious from what you've said that the key to breaking these Utes is this man Fontana. We get our hands on him and their resistance will collapse. Obviously, they believe him to be a leader of substantial importance or they wouldn't give him that kind of authority. Spring is coming. The high country will soon be rid of deep snow, and I can take a force large enough to deal with them on two fronts if need be."

"You, sir?"

"Yes, captain, me. I'll lead this expedition myself, and I won't walk into the kind of trap you did. When I'm done with this half breed and his friends I'll have them dancing at the end of a rope, and that includes Dull Knife too. That's the only thing those savages understand. What you always must remember, is that they are Stone Age people up against us, machine age man. The simplest things we take for granted can mystify them to awe, and when I give them a taste of our 12-pound cannons, they'll see how hopeless their cause really is, whatever they think that may be. The president and congress want all the northern tribes to sign peace and land treaties, and that's precisely what I mean to do. Now go give your men and animals a rest, while I get messages out for more troops and supplies. We've got time on our side. The longer we wait, the easier the high country will be to get into."

"Sir . . . will I be your second in command?" Cutter almost hated to ask, but had to.

"I'll have to think on that, Mr. Cutter. After what happened to you, I'm just not sure right now. You're dismissed."

Kyle was certain that when the horse soldiers returned to their headquarters and reported the beating they'd taken at his hands, General Cutter had mentioned they would surely mount a campaign against him and the Utes. Accordingly, as soon as he was sure the cavalry had departed the mountains, he made a fast, hard three day ride to reach Riverton in the black of night, then broke into Brady's old store and directed the braves to clean out the place of rifles and ammunition. An hour later they melted back up into shadowy timber and were gone long before daylight when the new owner, Josh Denton, opened up and saw the disarray of debris scattered across the floor and back store room. If there was only someone he could tell, but the little log town had no sheriff or law of any kind, as Kyle Fontana rode higher into the mountains with enough weapons now to arm many warriors and become an even more formidable force.

True to his word, three weeks later General Whitehead had the two regiments he'd requested and the supplies to begin his move north, deciding to make Riverton his base of operations. When they reached there after a nine day forced march, Denton was one of the first to come to him and tell of the robbery, a troubling revelation for the general and boldness even he didn't expect from the Utes.

"It's that Fontana. He's the only one smart

enough to pull off something like this." He was thinking out loud as the proprietor stood before him, then he looked up. "Thank you for that information distressing as it is. It's damned important that I know it. There's nothing I can do about your lost goods, but it's possible I may be able to buy some other supplies from you depending on how long this campaign lasts."

After dinner Whitehead assembled his officers and laid out his plan to move up into Ute territory.

"We'll ride out of here together but once we reach the area where Captain Cutter, here, encountered the Indians I'm going to divide us up into two units. I want you, Captain Meeker, to take charge of half the men and use your Cherokee trackers to try and find Dull Knife's main village."

Cutter's face dropped at the choice.

"I'll take Mr. Cutter with me as my second, and we'll flank you several miles out but keep in touch if anything important comes up through our scouts. If you are able to locate the village don't attack on your own. Instead, notify me and we'll have them between us before we move in. The last thing these savages think is that we'll be up in here looking for them. Surprise is our main advantage so long as we use it wisely. Now, bring in those Cherokees so I can explain to them precisely what I want them to do, and you stand by just in case they don't completely understand what I'm saying. You do speak some Cherokee, don't you?"

"I do, sir."

"Good. Fetch them up. When I'm done with them we'll turn the men in for a good night's rest because it may be the last one any of us get for a while." And at the moment the general could not know just how prophetic his words would be.

The slow, meticulous search into high country stretched into one week, then two, as the horse soldiers grimly stuck to their task with only the glimmer of old trails to follow, yet Whitehead would not be deterred. Instead of dejection and exasperation, the thought that this strange white man, Kyle Fontana, actually had a hand in leading the Utes drove him on. He'd have him no matter what, and finally almost at the end of the third week he got the break he'd been praying for.

Dark Eyes, one of Meeker's Indian scouts, was out early one morning when he saw just the faintest whisp of camp smoke rising up in a thin tendril over a timbered ridge nearly a mile away. He turned his pony toward it, stopping just under a knife-edged saddle where he slipped down and crept to the top peeking slowly over. A quarter mile below, set in a big meadow with a small creek winding through on one edge lay the main Ute camp, still quiet as everyone slept. After a quick count of the lodges, and number of horses picketed near the creek, he melted back down and quickly led his horse away at a walk until he was sure he was safe, then leaped atop the pony and headed back for Meeker's camp at a flying run.

When the captain received word of the fantastic find he sent two scouts to retrieve General Whitehead, and less than two hours later, the combined force was mounted and already closing in. When they reached the valley only a few Utes were outside their lodges as the general surveyed the scene, then whispered orders to Meeker and Cutter.

"We'll split up here. I want you to take your men and circle around the far end of the valley, while we stay here. Once you're in position give me a signal with your mirror and we'll ride down on them from two directions." He ordered Meeker, then turned to Cutter.

"I want you to take a dozen men and get to those Indian ponies while we attack. Run them off before the Utes can get to them. If we can keep them on foot they won't have a chance, and we can cut them down. Both of you keep your eyes open for this Fontana. I especially want him alive if at all possible, do you understand? I don't want him killed. I have other plans for him in front of a gallows. Now, get going and stay clear of this ridge so you're not seen. Hurry, while we've still got the edge."

Half an hour later, Quiet Moon had exited her lodge and just filled a gourd with water from the creek, when she looked up to movement on the distant ridge and saw the strange figures of mounted men as they whipped their horses down at breakneck speed into a full charge. Instantly, she dropped the container and ran for the lodge shouting a warning as she went.

"Kyle, Kyle, horse soldiers are coming! Quick, warn the others!"

He heard her shouts, exiting the teepee rifle in hand but not fully understanding until he turned and saw the first wave of cavalrymen come thundering onto flat ground streaking for the village as muffled rifle shots rang out, and more braves spilled from their lodges caught by surprise, diving back inside for weapons. Now more shots turned him in the opposite direction as Whitehead and his troopers came flashing in at the other end of the valley catching them in a withering crossfire, as Kyle yelled for Quiet Moon to run for the teepee while he took several braves and made a mad dash for the horses as the two lines of blue-coated troopers reached each other in the village center then wheeled their animals around firing indiscriminately at anyone that moved as Utes ran in fear, confusion, and sudden death.

Out of the corner of his eye Kyle saw Dull Knife also running for the ponies then Cutter and his men closing in fast as the chief pointed and yelled for help. When Kyle realized he couldn't reach the remuda first he skidded to a stop, swinging his rifle and firing on Cutter, whose horse went down screaming, throwing him through the air to land stunned for a moment until he regained his senses and rolled up to his feet, suddenly aware of Fontana advancing on him through the acrid haze of blue gun smoke at a dead run.

"You!" he screamed, fumbling for the snap flap on his holster, frantically trying to pull the pistol free and barely clearing leather as Kyle crashed into him both men rolling on the ground wrestling to turn the weapon on each other, with first Kyle on top then Cutter grunted face to face.

But now Kyle regained the top and this time the captain could not throw him off as he levered the black barreled pistol lower and lower, slowly turning it in Cutter's hand until their bodies came together to the muffle crash of a single shot.

For a moment neither man moved, locked in a killing embrace, then slowly the buckskin victor pulled himself off the dying officer to stand under heaving shoulders and look around at the chaos still raging around him. Then suddenly Snow Ball came into view and he hailed the big horse, grabbing his rifle out of the tall grass and leaping on his back to ride back into the swirling mass of red men, horse soldiers, and screaming women and children running wildly in every direction as gunfire continued unabated, with the cavalrymen clearly winning the lopsided battle.

Suddenly, up on the ridges, Red Star and a large party of Ute hunters that had been out several days meat hunting, saw the raging battle below and quickly kicked their ponies down to sweep in behind the unsuspecting troopers, turning the entire scene from one of sure victory to instant slaughter, streaking among them firing nearly at point blank range as blue coats fell from the saddle in complete confusion.

Finally, Whitehead, at the far end of the village realized what was happening and ordered his bugler to blow retreat and regroup. As he and his men kicked their horses off the flats up into first timber they were pursued by fast-closing warriors who did not stop until the troopers reached the topmost ridge then dismounted to fire back down from cover, breaking off the pursuit as the Indians turned back for the bottoms.

All the rest of that day, both sides sniped at each other from long range with neither side mounting another charge as they took count of their dead and rearmed their fighters. Then, near sundown, the general had his men pull off and retreated under the cover of darkness well back into the mountains for fear the Utes would rally and try to attack them at night. After a two-hour ride, he posted sentries, then took stock of the situation under a hastily thrown up tent command post, as his doctor tended the wounded and dying.

"I've never seen Indians fight like that before, and I've fought my share over the years," he mused, lighting a cheroot and sitting heavily on a canvas chair. "Just when we were about to finish them off." He looked up at his battled-scarred officers.

"It's their rifles, sir. Without those weapons we would have wiped them out just like you said this morning, but now they're as well armed as we are," one lieutenant offered.

"Yes, those damned rifles, I believe you're right about that. Where in God's name do you suppose..." Then he remembered the store back in Riverton that was cleaned out.

"Fontana... he probably had a hand in this, nobody else in their right mind would sell rifles like that to those savages. Did any of you see him during the fight? Anyone get a shot at him, or think they hit him?"

The men only shook their head in grim silence.

"We lost Captain Cutter," Meeker announced. "I saw his body when we rode out, but I couldn't do anything about it the way we were fighting to save ourselves. We didn't pick up any of the dead, sir. We just couldn't or there would be a lot more of us back there. I'm sorry."

"Has anyone made a count on our losses?" Whitehead hated to ask even as he spit the words out.

"I believe the count is... fourteen killed, and twenty-one wounded, sir, but we still have men right here that are in trouble. There's no telling what might happen by morning."

Whitehead didn't answer as he looked down

thinking, exhaling a cloud of smoke, rubbing the back of his neck.

"That bastard Fontana... I'll hang him if it's the last thing I do. If he wants to take sides with those savages then I'll treat him just like them when I get my hands on him, and I WILL get him, even if I have to extend my command here right up to my retirement!"

"And how about the Utes? Does anyone have a figure on how many we killed, any kind of an idea at all?" He tried again.

"No sir... I did see a number of women and some children... among the dead but don't have a count on bucks though I'm sure our first charge took down plenty of them." Meeker hesitated, looking around the circle of men. "You did say to kill everyone didn't you general, even women and children?"

"That's correct, Mr. Meeker. That's exactly what I said. Our job here is to subjugate these wild people by any means possible and war, all out war, is one of the most effective ways to do this. Don't any of you let yourself get squeamish over it. If you'd seen the wagon train massacres I have, I absolutely guarantee you you'd never give it a second thought. Remember what the Good Book says, gentlemen; "An eye for an eye, and a tooth for a tooth." Give as well as you get and don't go to your cot each night thinking or worrying about it. We've got a western continent to civilize just as we've done back east although it appears this man Fontana has lost his mind and gone the other way. But I'll set him straight on the gallows. Now, in the morning I want Dark Eyes and another scout to go back and reconnoiter the village while we pull back to Riverton for more supplies and troops. Tell him to meet us there, Mr. Meeker. The next time we find Dull Knife and his white friend they'll be no more surprises. We'll outnumber then and finish them off with more blue coats than they ever knew existed!"

But when the Cherokee snuck carefully up to the top ridge the next morning and peered down into the hidden valley, he found it totally abandoned with only the stripped and naked bodies of the soldiers killed yesterday spread across green grass. During the night the entire Ute camp had packed up and melted back into even higher mountain country to regroup and hold an important council about the strategy to come. Kyle asked to speak that night.

"The horse soldiers cannot live off the land as you do, for they must always bring all their supplies in with them to fight. When they are gone they must return to the valleys for more. Long as we move back and make them use up their food and ammunition they will always turn away after a big fight. We were lucky Red Star returned when he did or we all might lay back in the valley along with the horse soldiers. Neither you or I asked for this war, but now that it has started I must speak the truth. It will be a long one that requires all the strength we have. The horse soldiers will bring more men against us now that they know they cannot win easily. Dull Knife once asked me when I first came to you if I would stand with the Utes and fight my own people. Now, you've seen that I have, but I must tell you I take no pleasure in it even though I knew it had to be done. I wanted both you and me to live in peace, but the cavalry would not stop. We are in for a long, hard fight that will not be easy. Steel yourself for what is to come, my brothers."

That night after council, Kyle lay in his teepee with Quiet Moon slowly rubbing his back without speaking, until she leaned down whispering in his ear.

"Why are you so quiet, Ky-le? You spoke well at council tonight."

He continued staring into the pulsing flame of the firepit without answering for a long time until she kissed him lightly on the neck and he finally rolled over staring up at her as his hands lifted to cup her face gently.

"I was thinking that I came here to find peace, and instead I've found a war that could finish all your people. The life both you and I have always known will never be again, now. I'm not sure the others or even Dull Knife really understood what I said. They'll have to fight for their lives to survive after yesterday. The cavalry won't stop, not now, not after the beating they've taken. They'll come back with more and more . . ."

"But if you did not come here we would not have found each other, would we?" she countered, her eyes boring deep into his, as she tried to massage the worry lines off his deeply tanned face.

"Yes, that is true, but that makes it even harder, because now I have you to worry about too, as well as your people. For once I'm not sure I can do it all."

"But you have Dull Knife and all his warriors . . ."

"Wait . . . listen to me, Quiet Moon, and try to understand what I'm saying. The horse soldiers can always go back to their home and get more men no matter how many are killed or wounded, but Dull Knife cannot. When he loses a warrior there is no one to replace him.

Do you see what I mean? This war will be a war of attrition."

She put a finger to his lips silencing him for a moment.

"What does . . . att-trit—ion mean?"

He had to smile now, then pulled her pretty face down to his, kissing her on the mouth, holding her there for a moment longer.

"It means it will be a long, long fight that could last many moons and even many seasons. That may be a war your people cannot win. Can you see that?"

Slowly, she laid down beside him snuggling close, her head on his chest digging slender arms under him and hanging on tightly.

"Do not think of it anymore, Ky-le. I will not let you. Hold me here by the fire and think only of us and what we have that lies ahead, for it will be good, it must be good."

"I do, darling." He worked his hands deep into her long, black hair, caressing her neck. "Believe me, I do more than you'll ever know."

But as Fontana predicted throughout that long summer the horse soldiers came back under General Whitehead to engage them two more times in major battles without a clear winner, primarily because Kyle had convinced Dull Knife to send runners throughout the Ute nation to recruit more braves to send against the white invaders. The bitter stand-offs only further infuriated the general, but if he was beside himself with his failure to clearly win a victory, Dull Knife also had his own problems to face. Trying to keep so many warriors all in one place and under a single command, his, and feed them only made his alliance tenuous at best and especially as time wore on toward fall, when many of the tribes would have to move into lower country again.

But then a strange and unpredictable thing happened that not only electrified the chief and all his Indian army, but also all other tribes that heard of it. It was a story spreading fast throughout the Indian nations of a great and powerful medicine man risen far to the west in the Paiute country near a vast desert lake. He'd had a stunning vision of victory for all Indian peoples against the white man wherever he was found, for in a deep trance he'd seen himself rise and begin a long journey east toward the Rocky mountains, and everywhere he went the souls of dead red men rose up behind him to take their place at his side in a growing, unstoppable army. Then even the ghost buffalo slaughtered by whites came up from green grass to dance and pound their feet in a thunder that could be heard for a hundred miles in every direction, shaking the earth with ten million slashing hooves. Any and all that stood before those overpowering forces would fall like ripe wheat to the swish of a razor-edged scythe. And the magical man who could summon up these long dead spirits was simply called Wovokwa.

Chapter Seven

Wovokwa

When Dull Knife summoned him to his lodge, Kyle could tell from the older man's eyes and voice that he was extremely excited about something and in a way he'd never seen before from the usually stoic Ute. After sitting, he neglected the usual formalities and instead got right to the point of his invitation.

"Ky-le. Have you heard of this medicine man who is called Wovokwa, and his great power over all who stand in his way?"

Fontana nodded slowly without answering, for he had heard something about it but only considered it a myth, even though it was something Indian people often placed a lot of faith in.

"It is told that he will come here to our country but I fear he will be too late to help us in our battles with the horse soldiers. He lives far away where the sun sets and would take many moons to reach this land. I have already talked with my chiefs who agree we should send a messenger to him and ask that he come to help us. We have agreed that you are the one to deliver it. I want you to find him and show him the way here. You have already done much for us, and I know your heart is true and can be trusted as if you were one of us. And, a white man asking for this would show how much power we have that you chose the Ute way of life. I know this journey will pass through the lands of our enemies, but still I must ask you to go. I am told Wovokwa even speaks the white man's tongue, and that makes you more important in his eyes. Will you take Short Bull and go as I ask?"

For a moment Kyle couldn't answer as he struggled with the enormity of such a request. Even if this Wovokwa really did exist, he was reputed to live nearly nine hundred miles away on a treacherous journey that could take a month or more if he could complete it. Slowly, as he regained his senses, he reached out and placed a hand on the chief's shoulder.

"Dull Knife, what you ask of me is to leave my woman, leave this village that I now call home, and leave you to fight the cavalry on your own. Can this man really be that important to risk all this on just a rumor of other tribes? What if he does not exist at all, and this is just the talk of loose tongues? Let him come to us if he is so powerful a man. Then if he does possess the powers you speak of he can use them to help us."

"We do not have the time, Ky-le. I have lost many warriors already, and others talk of returning to their villages before winter comes again and they must move their women and children. You and Short Bull can ride steady and find this man I seek. The sooner you go, the sooner you will return. I know that I ask much from you, but still I must. Will you go Ky-le?"

Fontana's shoulders dropped as he sighed in resignation. He knew the Indian mind well enough to realize that once a story like this fixes itself upon red men they refuse to believe it is not true, always looking for some Spirit sign to return and help them in times of need. There was no arguing against it as he got to his feet, looking down at the old man.

"I want to talk to Quiet Moon first, then I will give you your answer."

"Quiet Moon was made as our own daughter, but she should have no word to keep you here. This is a man's decision and not a woman's."

For the next two days she fiercely argued against Kyle leaving, even going so far as to plead that they both take what they had and leave together for some other place far away from the attacks and constant moving of the village after each battle.

"Please, Ky-le. Do not do this thing. We have a life to live too. Let Dull Knife send someone else. I do not want to take the chance of losing you on a journey so far away into a land no one here knows."

Her lips trembled in fear and her eyes filled with tears that ran down her cheeks unashamedly, as he pulled her close trying to comfort her.

"I have to go, Quiet Moon. Dull Knife is convinced this Wovokwa is the only one who can save him and his people against the horse soldiers. Nothing I can say will change his mind, I've already tried. Please, don't cry. Instead, pray for my return as soon as possible. Short Bull and I will be as careful as we can. Try to understand, I must do this for him."

On the morning he was ready to leave, she took off the blue stone amulet she always wore around her neck, slipping it over his, then tucking it inside his buckskin shirt.

"My love is in this necklace, and it will bring you back safely to me. Do not take it off or my spirit will lose its hold on your heart. Come back to me Ky-le. I will be waiting."

They kissed once tenderly then stepped outside the lodge where Short Bull, the chief, and a large gathering of warriors stood waiting. One more long look at her, and Kyle swung atop Snow Ball as Dull Knife stepped forward with one final word of departure. Then they pulled their horses around, riding slowly down the length of the village until disappearing into thick pines at the far end, each man wondering if this would be the last time they'd see the village and their loved ones in it.

Now, the first freezing cold nights of autumn returned and with it intermittent snows lacing all the high country, only a prelude of what was to come. In two weeks the pair rode down into lower hill country and out onto the vast sagebrush flats of a high desert. In another week they crossed a high range of mountains beyond which they found a seemingly endless lake whose shores were caked in thick salt, along with the Indians that lived just back of the waves. Surprisingly they did not attack once they heard of their journey for they, too, had heard the electrifying name of Wovokwa and the immense powers he was said to possess.

After a brief stay and resupply, they skirted the huge body of water for another four days until it ended in a rising series of black rock plateaus devoid of trees and only carpeted in gray-green sagebrush for as far as the eye could see, while winter's icy hand gripped the barren vistas even more bitterly. The pair wrapped themselves in fur capes and hats, then double-lined buckskin pants and boots trying to keep out the cold. But it cut through them as if they had on nothing, and several times each day they had to stop and get down, dancing a jig and pounding gloved hands into each other trying to bring back some semblance of warmth. How could anyone live in this land, let alone a supposed messiah, they wondered?

It took two more weeks to span the high desert and finally ride up on a shallow, half-frozen creek lined in scraggly cottonwoods that meandered farther west where they met the first band of suspicious, southern Paiutes, warlike and stand-offish until Fontana mentioned the name of Wovokwa, and they pointed the pair west again, then south on a branch of the small desert waterway crossing over sand mountains. Finally, up ahead they could see the faint shimmer of another desert lake in the weak winter sun.

Arriving at its steep, terraced shores, small bands of Indians were found living in caves and simple stick huts who directed them to its far end. On the final day they rode up to a single, large stone lodge with many horses tethered out front, and after getting down they walked around back to find a big gathering of red men sitting in a circle warmed by a crackling fire. In the circle center a tall Indian bedecked in ceremonial buckskins stopped talking as the pair came into view and all heads turned to appraise the newcomers. Suddenly realizing one was white by his thick growth of beard and mustache, several leaped to their feet in alarm until Kyle spoke out in Ute.

The big man ordered them to sit back down. He strode forward slowly fixing his gaze on the strange looking pair and aiming his feathered staff at Kyle as he came to a stop nearly face to face and demanded to know who they were and why a white man would dare come to this place at this time. Speaking slowly, Kyle explained his mission and message from Dull Knife while everyone listened. When he was done, the man's gleaming gaze bore into him for several moments longer until he finally pointed to a place in the circle and told them to sit. Without asking, Kyle knew, at last, he was in the presence of the man he'd ridden nearly a thousand miles and over a month to find, the great Indian mystic, Wovokwa.

For the next three days all listened to the mesmerizing tale of his vision as even more Indian emissaries from other tribes trickled in to take their place and wonder at the power this strange man must possess. Then finally Kyle had the chance to speak to him alone, once more explaining Dull Knife's plight and that of the Utes.

"My chief wants you to come with me back to our country and use your great powers to stop the horse soldiers that grow in numbers each time we fight. He believes you can do what no other man can, and is certain you can save the Ute nation if you'll follow me there."

"You are a white man fighting against your own people? What kind of man would do such a thing? I have to wonder if you really speak the truth."

"Why I do what I do is of little concern. I have my reasons and they mean nothing compared to the army of red men you've promised will rise up to follow you when you ride east.

If you are as powerful as you say, then come with me back to the high country and fulfill your destiny with people that need and believe in you. If you do not, they will think you are weak."

Wovokwa stared at this strange white man who dared challenge him without answering for several moments. Then he began.

"I cannot leave before the Great Spirit tells me it is time. Maybe in spring when the land is warm again I shall begin my journey but not now, not in the heart of winter. Go tell your chief these are my words and await my arrival."

"Spring is too late. He needs you now. If you do not come he will know your vision was not true, and all the words you've spoken here are only carried away by the wind, not for the ears of men!"

"You are a white man living in an Indian world. Even though you know the red man's tongue, you do not know of our ancient ways. I did not ask you to come here, and now that you have you try to tell me not to listen to spirit voices of my father and all fathers before him? Only a fool would listen to you. Go back to the Ute chief and tell him what I have said. I will have an army no white army can stand against. Do not talk to me anymore of what

YOU want, Font-ana. You still have a white man's heart and cannot understand what I possess for my people."

Kyle stood staring at the medicine man without answering, and even though he knew Wovokwa could not produce the spirit army he'd promised, he also understood that once Dull Knife realized he would not return with him, it might just be enough to melt away his resolve to fight off the increasing numbers of cavalrymen sent against him and spell the downfall of the entire Ute nation.

Then the next day when he prepared to start the long ride back to the high country, Short Bull surprised him by saying he would not leave but intended to stay and listen to more of Wovokwa's wondrous stories and glory to come. Kyle started to argue with him but realized the Ute sub-chief had fallen under the spell of the powerful medicine man and nothing he could say or do would change his mind."

"Tell Dull Knife I will return with Wovokwa and his spirit army of many braves when he is ready. And let my woman and young sons know there will be no more white soldiers when we return."

If the long journey to find the Indian seer was perilous, the trip back through growing winter became a brutal and lonely struggle just to exist, as arctic winds howled across open sagelands, freezing everything in its icy breath. Even the big spotted horse began to slow to the rigors of numbing cold, turning his tail to the wind as Kyle huddled low on his broad back and made more frequent stops each day, trying to build a smoky sagebrush fire and extract what little heat it offered.

It took almost a week longer to reach the salt lake and its wind-driven waves slapping along a frozen shore, only to find the Indians once there had moved back into the protection of surrounding foothills leaving only a few fish heads and dried out waterfowl carcasses in their wake. Kyle rested for two days boiling the remaining skin and bones into a foul-smelling mush to help supplement his fast dwindling supplies, then ate it while holding his nose. When he rode out the great wall of mountains crossed earlier was now a jagged silhouette of frozen white, and for two more days he tried to find another way across but could not until he found an old elk trail coming down from the tops and turned Snow Ball up.

That night he rested in a small stand of quaking aspen, and at dawn stoked his wet wood fire back to life and ate a little snow for moisture but nothing else. Then he was in the saddle climbing higher still. By the third day the big horse was struggling through drifts nearly belly deep until Kyle piled off, trying to help by leading him. But only broke through himself, floundering for hours until his strength gave out and the blinding snowfields made his eyes ache with pain as he squinted for a way through.

Near dark he reached thinner crust along a windblown ledge and pulled himself into a shallow cave after tethering his horse nearby. He was soaked to the skin and frozen from head to toe with no fire and nothing to burn to help, shivering through a fitful sleep. When he awoke, the dawning sky was a blanket of silent snow falling in big flakes that built up quickly as he pulled himself to his feet and urged Snow Ball ahead in a direction he wasn't even sure of anymore, the world around him blotted out in a thick curtain of snow.

Many hours later he was aware that the horse had stopped in the lee of a few pitiful dead snag trees and he half slid, half fell to the ground, staggering toward a small pile of branches to crawl under for what little protection they offered. As he lay there he tried to remember how many days it had been since he'd left the medicine man far to the west, but he couldn't. His mind and body were frozen to inaction, and if he didn't get a fire going soon he wouldn't need one at all, freezing to death without ever waking up again, but he didn't have the strength to gather limbs or strike his fire steel. Maybe this was how death felt? Maybe he should just accept it, lost in a world of endless snows and zero temperatures where nothing could live. Slowly his eyes closed. Vaguely he thought of Quiet Moon. He'd never see her again and he loved her so much, but now she would be lost to him forever, and there was nothing he could do about it. Then everything went black.

Sometime later that night his quivering body stirred ever so slightly as a thread of consciousness moved him to open his eyes. He tried but could not, frozen shut until slowly, painfully with shivering fingers he pried one open. It must have stopped snowing, but the bitter world of frozen night was still empty and devoid of form. He wondered if he was dead or alive, then suddenly he thought he saw a tiny, wavering outline coming closer and closer and the ghostly image grew until it became the transparent form of a man, an Indian man, and as it brightened . . . Wovokwa!

Kyle tried to sit up but could not, frozen in a fetal position as first fear then wonderment gripped his rigid body. The image seemed to be trying to talk as its mouth moved but no voice came out and it drifted closer until it hung nearly over the top of him as he reached up trying to touch it but passed through nothing but air. Then it slowly lifted an arm pointing off into the night and looking back down at Fontana until finally he could just barely hear it speak as if on a distant wind.

". . . that way . . . Font-ana . . . go . . . that way . . ."

Suddenly the image wavered, losing its intensity, then began to fade away like a dying fire.

"Wa—it." Kyle could only croak a single word, but it was too late, the figure flickering off into darkness and was gone.

Somehow, some way, through super human strength he fought to get to his frozen feet and stand, reeling like a drunk, groping around in the dark for the horse until he found it just yards away shivering in deep snow. He gripped the saddle horn, fighting to lift a foot into the stirrup while Snow Ball stood patiently waiting until he did, then struggled even harder to pull his tattered body up into the saddle. With his last ounce of strength he reined the animal off in the direction Wovokwa, or whatever it was, had directed, then collapsed, head down, moving off into the night.

Many hours later he awoke with a start when the horse slipped badly on loose shale, skidding down a rocky chute until it regained its feet on more level ground. It must be after dawn, the blurred images around him turning themselves into tall pines when his eyes cleared a little, the ground here only splotched with occasional patches of white under the snow line. He looked up at the boiling storm clouds far above as the sudden realization set in that somehow he made it, he was alive, alive by God! He could even feel his hands and feet for the first time in days and painful as they were at least they still worked.

He pulled the horse to a stop and built a fire, flames leaping to life from the stack of dead sticks and limbs, then curled up next to it thinking the whole thing over again. He'd come through a white hell and survived. He still couldn't believe it, then he remembered the ghostly visitor that directed him to safety. Had it all only been the delirious dream of a dying man, or somehow had the mystical medicine man come to him in the black of night willing him to live? For a long time he just lay there thinking about it, then finally fell into the first real sleep he'd had in nearly a week, soaking up the life-giving warmth.

The days plodding steadily east across the

high desert came and went in uncounted monotony except for the misery of blistering hands and feet, but he knew now he'd make it back to Quiet Moon no matter what. Would Dull Knife still keep the village up high waiting for his return, or move down into lower country? He wasn't sure after all this time but eventually he reached familiar foothills and climbed higher toward the mountain hideaway. He was still weak after the torturous ordeal, but the valiant horse carried him forward as they finally neared the end of their long, long journey.

Then one day he topped a ridge to look down on the village, blue smoke twisting up from every lodge in a land of winter white. For just a moment his breath caught in his throat, the realization that his bitter journey was almost over, as he urged Snow Ball over the edge and down.

Someone below saw the lone rider and yelled a warning as Dull Knife and the others spilled from their teepees, rifles in hand to watch the stranger slowly wind his way down through thick timber until reaching the bottom, then ride out into the open at the far end of the village. Instantly, Quiet Moon recognized the spotted horse and broke into a run while the rest of the village followed.

"Ky-le, Ky-le!" she yelled, tears in her eyes as she reached him, grasping his hand and leading him back to the lodge where he slowly lowered himself to the ground and she got her first good look at him.

"What happened to you, Ky-le, are you all right?" She wrapped her arms around his tattered clothes as he fought to keep his feet and Dull Knife came up.

"You have returned as I knew you would. Did you see the medicine man Wovokwa? Does he carry the spirit power we have heard of? Can you talk to me of it, Font-ana?"

But the buckskin man could only whisper a reply before completely collapsing.

"Yes ... I have seen him ... he has the power you seek ... but I do not think he will come soon. Can we speak of it later ... I must rest now." And Dull Knife nodded, appraising his pitiful condition before turning away with troubling thoughts of his own.

Once inside he fell in a heap and the woman covered him in thick, warm fur robes, leaning down to study his gaunt face and heavy beard as she ran fingers delicately across his cheek.

The pain etched there was obvious, but Kyle Fontana had made nearly a two-thousand mile journey and come home. For now all that mattered was he was back safely in her arms.

Chapter Eight

The Pipe of Peace?

Back in Riverton General Whitehead had exchanged a series of letters with the War Department's general staff in Washington, and their exasperation at his inability to bring the Utes to their knees was obvious as he read the final lines of the latest communiqué.

"If you cannot subjugate this nation either by signing a peace treaty or, failing that, accomplish their final defeat by early spring, it is our intention to replace you with another officer. As you're fully aware, many of the southern tribes have already been removed from their original lands and sent to reservations. There is no reason to delay this procedure with these northern Indians, for the longer they are able to resist the more emboldened they will become. Accordingly, we are sending you two more regiments from our southern command to complete this order. Use them wisely in the shortest possible time. The westward expansion of civilization cannot be halted by just one tribe, in this case the Utes, or any others we may encounter.

I remain,
Lawrence A. Donnely
Secretary of War"

The general sat back in his chair, closing his eyes for a moment while rubbing his temples in thought. These damn Utes and the white man that helped lead them. He was certain that if it wasn't for him, Dull Knife and the rest of his tribe would have fallen long ago, but just maybe the command back in Washington sitting in leather chairs on their fat rear ends, finally had one good idea after all. Instead of the long, dangerous excursions into the high country trying to root out the Indians and always with a loss of good men hard to replace, why not call for a peace treaty? It was something he'd simply never thought of, engaged as he was in trying to defeat them militarily, but now it suddenly seemed crystal clear. Yes, that was the answer, bring them in for a treaty and right under his thumb!

He called a staff meeting of his officers, detailing the new plan to them and instructing Captain Meeker to use his two lead Indian scouts, Dark Eyes and Kicking Bear, to take enough provisions and search for Dull Knife under a flag of truce with a handwritten message from him personally to come in and meet in Riverton.

"How can we be sure the Utes won't just kill before they get the chance to even deliver your offer?" Captain Daniels, a new replacement, asked.

"We can't, captain. But even if they did we have other Cheyennes to use."

Daniels started to question the general's obvious callousness, new as he was to this post, as he looked around the table at the others who didn't seem a bit alarmed at Whitehead's attitude.

"You're new here Mr. Daniels, but you'll come to learn what your fellow officers already have. Namely, that life and death are a daily part of the western experience, and in the primitive world of the Indian, it means the chance to hobnob with their ancestors. They do not fear death, they welcome it without a shrug or word of protest. Besides, killing those two red men would take some considerable doing. They're both deadly fighters, even feared by their own people. There's no telling how many men they murdered before we engaged them as scouts and trackers. Now, Mr. Meeker, tell them what I want them to do while I write this 'invitation'." He smiled smugly at the men sitting around the table which they returned in kind, but the young officer wasn't through yet as he tried one more question obvious to him if no one else.

"General, how is Dull Knife going to be able to read your offer. You're writing it in English, aren't you?"

"He isn't. But Fontana will."

The scouts left Riverton the next day with only their winter garb and one pack mule for supplies, starting the long climb up into surrounding mountains as Whitehead stepped out on the porch for a moment to watch them go, puffing on one of his cigars. Then the chill of winter sent a shiver through his light jacket and he stubbed it out and went back inside, pleased with himself.

The two red men spoke little throughout the following days, seemingly able to read each other's mind as they doped out trails or pointed to some piece of country worth investigating, but always they rode with their rifles across their laps ready for instant action as they penetrated deeper and deeper into Ute country, and the land of their deadly enemies.

At night they built only the smallest fire even in these freezing temperatures so as not to be discovered, then at the first hint of dawn were saddled up and gone again on another long and careful day of riding. Meeker had once confided to the general that he'd take a dozen Cheyenne scouts over three times that number of troopers any day for scouting or ambushing their enemies and these two certainly exemplified that, though it was a statement he'd never utter in the presence of his own men.

Even though the captain had ordered the pair not to waste time going back to the camp where the great battle had taken place earlier that year, once on their own they did so anyway on the chance they might find some sign that the Utes had passed near here on later occasions. But when they entered the valley it was deserted except for the scattered bones of dead men both Indian and white, plus some tattered remnants of clothing. That's when they swung back to the west paralleling the great mountains but dropping down in elevation slightly where they thought a winter camp might be set up.

One morning two weeks later they rode through some particularly thick snow-laden pines only to exit the other side right into a party of Ute hunters, who quickly covered then disarmed them, tying their hands behind their backs and blind folding them and quickly returning back to camp two days away. When they reached the village there was an instant call for their death. But when Dull Knife and Fontana approached the pair Kicking Bear nodded continually for the pack sack atop their mule, and Kyle found the note wrapped in oil cloth. He read it, and when he was done he looked at the Cheyennes asking if either understood "American," but without a response. Then he turned to the chief and translated the offer to meet to talk peace, and he stepped forward nearly nose to nose with his hated adversaries speaking slowly in Ute, which they could understand, asking how far away the horse soldiers were as Dark Eyes mumbled a reply.

"Keep them tied and guarded until I decide what I will do." He ordered his braves, the pair taken to the center of the village and forced to sit, stakes driven behind their backs their hands retired to them.

"Come with me, Font-ana," he ordered as both men headed for his lodge.

Once inside Dull Knife was clearly interested in pursuing the possibility of meeting with the general but Kyle wasn't so sure arguing for more caution.

"Why would this Whitehead want to talk peace now, in the middle of winter when there is no fighting?"

"He and his horse soldiers have not been able to beat us. Maybe now he seeks peace because there is no other way?" the old man countered, but still Kyle was not convinced.

"Listen carefully to my words, Dull Knife. In the great valley where I once lived were other red men such as you, but the horse soldiers asked them to smoke the pipe of peace too and they lost all their lands, their horses, weapons, and dignity. They were sent far away to a place they did not know or want to go, penned like cattle. I tell you this offer for peace has two faces and one is turned away from you so you cannot see it."

The chief thought for a moment longer before answering, running a hand slowly across his face as he did so.

"You said with your own words that Wo-vokwa would not come back with you to help my people. If the white soldiers keep sending more and more men against us, I may not be able to turn them back as I have in the past. I have my women and children to think of, not just warriors, and I am not a young man anymore to ride and fight while the sun is in the air. I say let us talk to this white man and see what he offers, but I want you at my side when I do so, because you know the white man's heart if he talks true. Make the words on paper and tell him we will meet to blow a cloud of smoke, but offer him nothing more."

"I will do as you ask, but at least let me tell him we will not meet in Riverton where he has asked, for that is where all his strength lies. We must choose a spot that is safer... what do you think of the creek where the first white miners found yellow iron?" And Dull Knife agreed.

Kyle wrote the answer and the next morning the Utes led the scouts blindfolded again two days away from camp before turning them loose. Just before they parted he rode up alongside Dark Eyes, speaking slowly in Ute, handing him the reply.

"You tell this Whitehead that he comes only with four other officers and we will do the same. Tell him I will speak for Dull Knife, and he comes without weapons of any kind. Now go while you still have your hair."

The fierce-looking Cheyenne glared back at him with a look of contempt and scorn, then spit out four short words.

"You will die soon!"

And with that they pulled their ponies away and were gone in thick pines.

When the general read Kyle's reply he was ecstatic with joy they'd taken the bait, and quickly laid in plans to ambush the pair and capture both men at one time if they would not agree to a treaty of complete subjugation.

"What is the old saying, Mr. Meeker? You can catch more flies with honey than salt? Well, it appears we have some hungry for the taste of it, and I will serve it up thick enough to hold them right where I want them. Prepare the men to leave in the morning. When we come back we'll either have the Ute nation by the neck, or their two leaders roped over their own horses!"

Four days later when Whitehead and his officers arrived at Nugget Creek, he also had a dozen Cheyenne scouts carefully secret themselves out of sight surrounding the camp ready to pounce the moment he gave the signal, which would be him snubbing out his cigar in the dirt as they talked. Then they waited for Dull Knife and his party to show up.

It took another day before Dull Knife and

Fontana pulled to a stop atop the promontory looking down on the small figures of men and horses in camp below, but they had not come alone either, accompanied by a dozen well-armed warriors to take up positions half way down slope when the talks finally got started as insurance against anything unforeseen happening, a plan Kyle had insisted on from the very start. Then, as the horse soldiers saw them and signaled with a white flat to come in, the chief, Kyle, and two sub-chiefs started down after giving strict orders on what to do in case trouble developed.

"Sir, riders coming in!" one of the officers shouted as the general quickly exited his tent, eyes studying the Utes as they came closer and he quickly glanced around at his hidden scouts.

So, this was it at long last. He was finally going to get a look at this man called Fontana and the leader of the Ute nation all at one time. He stepped forward inhaling deeply as the four drew closer until his eyes settled on one man, the biggest physically, riding a black and white spotted horse. Without being told, he knew this was the white man who'd been his nemesis for so long, but he really wasn't prepared for his actual appearance.

He wore heavy buckskin clothes with a fur cape over his shoulder and fur hat above piercing gray eyes and full beard and mustache. His legs were adorned with knee-high leather boots embroidered with fancy beadwork, and even though his leather rifle scabbard was empty as the plan had been, he still carried a long knife on a decorated Indian's sheath and belt. Compared to him, Dull Knife was short and squat but powerful, his broad brown face decorated with scars of battles past, feathers adorning his long, black braided hair, and dressed in the same kind of detailed buckskins, the two sub-chiefs similarly dressed but not as fancy.

When the four pulled to a stop, the general still slightly awestruck, didn't quite know what to say until he caught himself clearing his throat and lifting a stubby hand in greeting.

"Ah . . . gentlemen . . . won't you step down? These are my officers Mr. Meeker, Mr. Bradly, and Mr. Daniels. We welcome you to our camp, and hope these talks will be fruitful. Do you prefer chairs or a blanket?" He swept a hand toward the canvas folding chairs lined behind him.

"We'll sit." Kyle answered, pointing out the strange contraptions to the Utes.

"Good then. Well, first of all I want to tell you how glad I am that you accepted my offer to talk peace. This is an important first step in ending hostilities before there is anymore loss of life. You don't mind if I smoke, do you?" He lit up a cigar offering them to the four men who shook their heads no.

"Are you translating for the others?" He raised an eyebrow to Kyle.

"That's right."

"That's fine, now let's get down to business. As a representative of the government of the United States and even the president if I might say so, I'm willing to offer you and all your people a new home where you'll be cared for, fed and housed, and for as long as you and your offspring live. They'll be a final end to constantly fighting and moving your village, and we may even be able to find you work of some kind, possibly growing hay or field crops, something like that? We may even be persuaded to let you keep your horses, if things work out peaceably..."

"Wait a minute." Kyle cut in. "Your offer was to talk about a possible peace settlement, not a total surrender of these people. They'll never hear of that."

Whitehead bristled at the interruption, face turning red as he leaned forward with narrowing eyes.

"Let me ask you something MR. FONTANA! Do any of these "friends" of yours speak even one word of English?"

Kyle shook his head no.

"Then I want to ask you one thing before I go any further, and it's just this. Why in the name of all that's holy did you end up as you have? What drove you to turn against your own people and take up with these ... these savages? They're little more than animals themselves, for God's sake, and that's how you've chosen to live your life!"

"What drove me? Men like you. I once scouted for the army and saw how they treated these people until I got a belly full of it. All they want is to be left alone, but what you've offered here is servitude, not peace. I won't council that."

"Can't you see you're fighting a war you cannot win, don't you understand that? These red men can't stand up under modern day cavalry and weapons. You've put your head in a hangman's noose helping them and fighting against your own race! Tell them to put down their arms and follow us out of these mountains, if you've got a shred of human decency left in you. You're not helping them, you're sealing their fate with this attitude of yours. You don't dictate the terms here, I do!"

Kyle looked into the general's small red eyes and knew the long trip here had been for nothing. Then he turned to Dull Knife, carefully translating Whitehead's demands, the old man's stoic face never changing as he listened with an unblinking stare. When he was finished he gave Kyle his answer as the general's patience wore thinner by the moment sitting there tapping his foot glancing nervously uphill again. Finally, Fontana turned to face him again.

"Dull Knife says he did not ask you to come here to his land and that of all his fathers. He says your white chief in Washington means nothing to him, and that he cannot give up what he does not own. The land, the animals, the sky belong only to the Great Spirit, and no man red or white. He did not choose to make war against any white man until the miners came into the Ute nation to dig for gold. So long as they stay in their log towns he does not care, but he will not have them violating his land. He wants you to keep them out of these mountains or there will be more fighting and more killing. If that happens the Ute nation will fight as long as there is a warrior left standing and many more men will die than already have. He asks if you remember the village fight where you lost many men?"

Whitehead's face was wrinkled with rage as he got to his feet glaring at both men, almost crushing the cigar still in his hand as he tried to control himself.

"You've just signed your own death warrant, do you know that? Go ahead, tell your "chief" what he's done. I gave him the chance to end this conflict and instead he spit in my face! Now we will do it my way, I'm tired of talking. You and your friends are under arrest. Stand up!" He threw the cigar to the ground, stamping it out. In the same instant Kyle said something quick and short to the Utes and they jumped to their feet, turning to run for their horses as the Cheyennes broke from cover running downhill and began firing.

Two Utes fell as the officers scattered for cover while the chief and Kyle reached the mounts, leaping into the saddle just as a bullet hit Dull Knife. They whipped their animals out of camp kicking hard for the cover of timber and up the steep trail. When they streaked out of harms way just under the rim, the Utes stationed there opened up on the pursuing Indians with withering rifle fire that sent them churning back downhill out of rifle range, as Fontana helped the old man off his horse.

"Where are you hit?" he shouted over the barking long guns, then saw the growing blossom of red soaking through his buckskins on his side, quickly peeling the shirt up trying to stem the flow of blood from the ugly wound.

"We must leave here quickly and get back to the village. Do you think you can ride?" he asked, and Dull Knife nodded, struggling back up to his feet, shouting orders over his shoulder for half the riflemen to remain behind and be sure the cavalry didn't follow, then head for camp after dark when they would not follow.

Over the next three weeks Dull Knife lay gravely ill, steadily tended by his wife and daughters plus Quiet Moon, Kyle, and the Ute medicine man, while General Whitehead marshaled his new forces for an all-out campaign to find and annihilate the Indians even while the waning days of winter were still at hand, and his reputation and career hung in the balance.

Then something happened that changed the whole scheme of events, one day when Quiet Moon took Kyle by the hand and led him into their lodge, turning to put both hands on his face, holding him there while they locked eyes.

"What is it, why do you look so serious?" he asked, kissing her lightly on the forehead, then pulling back to study her face.

"I have something to tell you Ky-le, something that will happen to change our lives, even though it comes at this hard time for all of us."

"Yes?"

"I am going to have your baby, Ky-le. I think it will come sometime in the summer."

Stunned and unable to speak as conflicting emotions of joy and concern rocked his mind, he recovered, pulling her close again, caressing her long, black hair, whispering in her ear.

"A child, darling . . . I once had little girls but I thought that life was over for me. Now you've brought it back and it makes me so happy I don't know what to say except I love you more than anything on this earth and will do everything I can to keep you and our growing child safe from whatever comes."

"I already know that, Ky-le. I put both of us in your strong hands for without you there is no life for me either."

But as she spoke those words, far away in Riverton General Whitehead had assembled his officers in front of a large wall map, pointer in hand as he began to speak.

"Up until now I've had to try and find, then engage the Utes with limited forces. That's going to change. With four new regiments I'm going to deploy you to fan out once we reach the high country until we find these renegades again. But once we do I do not, repeat DO NOT, want you to attack. Instead, hold your position and send scouts out to contact the rest of us. Then, when we meet I'll plan a coordinated attack with superior numbers and catch them in a trap they can't escape from. That's when we'll finish them off once and for all. This time, gentlemen, there will be no peace treaty, no bargaining, no mercy, and no prisoners. Now, prepare your troops for what lies ahead and prepare them well for it will not be easy, but victory is the only result I want and expect from each and every one of you and your men!"

Chapter Nine

Just Rewards

Almost three hundred miles west of the growing storm clouds of conflict, the two men who had actually started it all with their chance discovery of Indian gold, were living in the small desert mining town of Double Hot, unaware of the didactic forces they had set in motion, but not forgotten by at least one man.

Shane Irons was a U.S. Marshal who'd been meticulously dogging the pair's trail, following every lead he could dig up on Buck and Zinky, and his reputation as an iron-willed, determined lawman had not been an exaggeration. Irons was once the city sheriff who put down a wide-open cattle war between Jake Willis and Royal Dean's outfits over water and grazing rights back in Eagle Pass. He'd jailed half the cowboys from each ranch, then declared the town was off limits to anyone carrying a gun, and enforcing it with his famous sawed off 12-gauge shotgun in a Texas street shoot out with no less than Dean himself and killing him after taking a bullet from the cow man. From that day on he was known far and wide as the "shotgun sheriff," and his word was law.

His reputation grew to the point he eventually was offered the job as U.S. Marshal, which gave him the wide latitude to enforce the law anyplace and every place he thought it needed, whether in a state, territory, or wild country still untamed. His marshal's star was the backbone of his life, never married and a confirmed lifelong bachelor. When Shane Irons was given an assignment he'd stay on it until it was completed, one way or the other, and plenty had been completed at the end of his famous shotgun.

Now, he'd gotten a lead on the pair by questioning the owner of a small way station a month earlier who told him two men answering his description had stopped there and paid with gold nuggets for the supplies they'd bought instead of using cash. They'd also asked where the nearest town was, obviously strangers along the treeless, rock-strewn mountains edging the desert, but one rich in gold and silver ore and home to many hard rock mines.

"I told 'em Double Hot was about the next place in this part of the country," the store owner related. "One was tall, like you just said, the other a little man, sort of feisty like, know what I mean? Always jittering around, short little character that never stayed put for more than a second. I believe I heard the little man call his partner Buck, or something like that. They weren't here all that long, but they sure had enough gold to pay for anything they wanted, I could see that when the big man pulled out that leather pouch of his. They might have headed on up to Double Hot like I told'em, but I don't know that for sure."

Irons thanked the man and started for the town, arriving three days later to a dismal looking line of shacks warm even under the late winter sun, the strange formations on the hills back of it dug full of holes as miners probed and dug to find a rich vein of ore. The few men he saw on the dirt street made it clear his star-pinned presence wasn't exactly welcomed in this remote, wide-open jumble of businesses and one-room dwellings that had no sheriff much less even a church. Irons rightly concluded that even though it seemed nearly deserted by day, at night it would fill with men grimy from working in deep and dangerous shafts, and possibly some word of the men he was looking for around the five bars he'd already counted before pulling to a stop at the largest one.

Red Dog Saloon, the sign said, as he got down slapping dust from his clothes with a big Stetson. Then he stepped up the one stair entrance and went inside, three loafers at the bar turning to look him up and down as he came up and the owner, Red Haywood, walked down behind the counter as he polished a glass.

"What can I do for you?" he asked, eyeing the five-point star on Irons' vest. "You're a little far out to be playing lawman, aren't you?"

Irons ignored the remark and asked about Buck and Zinky.

"Never heard of 'em," Haywood shot back.

"I've been told they might have come this way. Are you certain about that? This isn't exactly New Orleans. What have you got, two hundred people in the whole place?"

"I don't keep count of who comes and who goes. Maybe they been here and left, I don't know. Besides, I'm not running a lost souls service, this is a bar. If you want a drink I've got that, if not I'll tend to other customers."

"All right, give me a shot of your best whiskey. Maybe someone else will come in who knows something. I'll just stick around for a little bit."

He poured the glass full as Shane took a sip, their eyes locking as he lifted the glass.

"That'll be four bits before you drain it."

Shane reached into his pocket, sliding the coins across the counter top, putting the glass down.

"Tastes like horse liniment."

"Then don't drink anymore of it. I guess you can stand here and hold up the bar, if you've got nothing else to do."

Haywood was obviously unhappy with his presence, and Shane wondered why, looking down the bar at the other men, asking them if they knew the two men he'd described, but they only shrugged and shook their head no. After a long pause he finished his whiskey.

"I'll be back."

And as he went out the door the others came together talking in low whispers.

"I think I might know the two he's talking about," one man said. "Don't they rent that cabin out by the Glory Hole mine?"

"Well, maybe, but don't go gettin' yourself mixed up in this. This lawman looks like nothin' but trouble." Haywood warned. "Anybody that would ride this far just to question two men would have to be half crazy himself, whatever it is they're supposed to have done!"

After dark that night a shadowy figure stepped silently down the street going from bar to bar but staying outside where he could study the faces through grimy windows without being seen, and also without success. Then, near midnight, he made one last swing ending at the Red Dog, where his attention was drawn to two men sitting in the back of the room while Haywood bent close talking to them. When he straightened up, Irons stepped even closer to the glass, studying them intently. They seemed to fit the description he'd gotten from both the Casper sheriff and the way station owner, but there was only one sure way to find out as he pushed through the door and the whole place suddenly grew quiet turning to face him.

"Get that shotgun outta here. I don't want no trouble in my place!" Haywood shouted, retreating from the two as Irons' eyes locked on both men and came slowly forward.

"You shut up and stay out of this," he ordered. "And that goes for the rest of you. You two. Stand up and lift those hog legs with your left hand real easy like. Drop them on the floor."

"Who in hell are you!" Buck got to his feet, black beard face bristling with alarm as his hands dropped to his side while Zinky stayed seated, eyes wide with terror, his hand slowly moving under the table for his holster.

"I'm a U.S. Marshal, and I want to talk to both of you about the killing of a man named Frank Brady, back in Riverton. Now, shuck those pistols. I won't tell you again!"

Buck bolted left, pulling his six gun, opening fire on Irons the same instant the shotgun spit flame and smoke, cutting him down while Zinky pulled the table up in front of him and fired blindly over the top until a second explosion of double 00 buck thudded through the wooden top and he was driven onto his back screaming in pain.

Irons lowered the shotgun pulling his .45 out and advancing slowly on the downed men, rolling Buck over with the toe of his boot, dead eyes staring up into space. Then he pulled the table from Zinky, who was still breathing but fading fast.

"He . . . would'a done . . . the same to . . . us." He labored, getting out the words.

"Who?" Irons asked, bending low to hear his small voice.

"Bra—dy. We . . . had'ta . . . do it, or he would'a took . . . it all." Then he sighed once and was gone.

Far beyond the deadly midnight drama of

Double Hot, even beyond the endless high desert of the Great Basin, Indian emissaries still rode west to see and hear the charismatic Wovokwa, and his fascinating tales of stunning victory over the white invaders. It was the largest and strangest Indian council ever to assemble, ancient mortal enemies suddenly come together to put aside tribal hatred in the common belief that this one all-powerful medicine man could galvanize them into one gigantic and invincible army.

But as spring drew nearer, Wovokwa's fame had spread even beyond the world of the Indian nations, for now the United States cavalry had also been warned of the red seer who lived by a desert lake and rode west to find him before he could stir up anymore trouble and resentment. When they drew near there was a violent pitched battle lasting nearly two weeks as the warriors retreated into surrounding mountains where they could hold off the troopers with the advantage of elevation and caves to secret themselves in while Wovokwa commanded them with the tactical genius of a West Point graduate knowing every nook and cranny to use to their advantage.

Eventually, the constant cannon fire directed on the Indians finally began to take its toll, and thirteen days later enough of them had either fled, been killed or captured, that they came down out of the hills and surrendered, lined up in a ragtag order and stripped of everything possible that could be used to fight with.

"Are we going to march them back to Fort McDermott, or just hang them?" A young sergeant asked Captain Horton, leader of the regiment.

"No, we're not going to do either. Instead, I'm going to give them back their horses now that they're defenseless. I want them to go back to their villages and tell their people what happened here, and how decisively they were beaten, and that their so-called "medicine man" is nothing more than a shame and fraud. I can't think of a better way to put an end to this charlatan than by the words of his own people. What they've really learned over the last two weeks is that the real Great Spirit comes out of the end of a pair of twelve-pound cannons, and not some hocus-pocus Paiute dressed up in beads and feathers! Now, I want him brought here in front of me where everyone can watch. Go get him, sergeant. It's time to teach these savages a lesson they'll never forget."

In a few moments the tall red man shuffled forward shackled hand and foot to stand before Horton.

"I'm told you speak some English. Do you understand what I'm saying?"

The red man stared for a moment then nodded his head slowly.

"I do," he answered.

"Good then. I want you to tell these Indians of yours that both they and you have been beaten and that you can do nothing about it, that you have no power to stop us, no great medicine, and that all your predictions were nothing but a pack of lies. Tell them it's over, they'll be no more talk of war. Go ahead."

Wovokwa's eyes never blinked as he leveled his gaze on the captain without answering or complying as Horton grew more and more impatient with each passing moment, tapping a stiff leather quirt against his boot, waiting.

"I said get to it, and I won't tell you again."

Still the Indian made no move to comply, and an instant later the captain lashed out viciously, the short leather whip cutting a deep gash across Wovokwa's face, and he reeled backwards but did not go down. Horton leaped forward to grab him by the shoulders and spin him around, facing the Indians and bringing the quirt down again and again on his back until finally he fell to his knees, but he would not cry out.

"Drag him over to that hitching post, and tie

his arms out spread eagle!" the captain demanded, as several troopers stepped forward to carry out the order. When they were done he stepped up measuring the distance with the whip, then drew back and began administering the rest of the savage beating until the red man hung helplessly, head down, and the officer finally stopped, sweat flowing, trying to catch his breath.

"Now, cut him down... and let him lay there. Don't touch him. I want the rest of them to remember what they've seen of their "precious" medicine man!"

"Will we be taking him back with us later, captain?" the sergeant inquired.

"No, there's no need for that now. He's not going to lead anyone anyplace. After we disperse this bunch you can drag him back to his shack." He stepped forward, leaning low to whisper in the Indian's ear.

"If I hear that you've made so much as a single word of war I'll personally come back here and hang you! I'll bet you understand that, don't you?"

But Wovokwa did not answer or move, even though his eyes were still open.

That night the red man lay in pain, his back cut to ribbons, as his woman tried to tend him, carefully washing away the blood with warm water, until finally he whispered for her to stop and leave him alone. Slowly he forced himself away from the pain and into a deepening trance reaching out into the black of night to the one man he knew he must find to help the Indians in their time of greatest peril. He may be physically beaten into a state of near helplessness, his gathering of warriors now scattered in every direction, but still he knew he must try to save what he could as he called on his greatest powers of concentration and spirituality, reaching out.

Kyle moaned something unintelligible in his sleep, then suddenly sat bolt upright, staring into the darkness of the lodge, sweat running down his face even though the fire next to him had long since burnt into cold, white ashes. It was that image of Wovokwa, the same one he'd seen up in the snow, but this time the voice was louder and clearer. He'd said that Kyle should immediately get up and warn the village that they must break camp and move away quickly because an impending attack was coming at dawn!

Quiet Moon stirred next to him then finally woke, her hand reaching up to comfort him.

"What . . . is it . . . Ky-le? Why are you breathing so . . . hard?"

"We . . . have to leave, soon as we can. I've

got to go tell Dull Knife. Something bad is going to happen if we don't."

"But what? What could happen? It is the middle of the night. We've seen no one for weeks."

"I just know it, that's all. Don't ask me why, just get up and start packing our things. I'll be back in a few minutes. Please, do it quickly."

It took nearly until dawn for the entire village to break camp and pack their protesting horses, and if it wasn't for his close friend's absolute insistence that they must go, Dull Knife would have ignored these demands from anyone else.

Two hours later when they topped a high ridge above the canyon camp, Dull Knife sent the rest of his people ahead while he, Kyle, and several chiefs stayed back, tying off their horses to lay on the rim and watch below. Then, just as the first rays of winter sun streaked through jagged peaks to the east, they saw three Cheyenne scouts come riding down through timber and tie off their horses to slide ahead on foot and creep to the canyon bottom searching for the Ute camp. Dull Knife slowly turned as he lay there looking into Kyle's eyes.

"Now I know you truly have the Great Spirit in your heart, but we must go before the horse soldiers find our tracks. Wovokwa could not come here to help us, but he talks through you. No white man's bullet can kill you anymore, for you have his power."

General Whitehead was infuriated at getting so close only to have the Utes slip away once again, and in his desperation he decided to split his forces in half, sending eight troops far and wide searching for the ever elusive, always moving Indians who paused to fight from ambush, inflicting heavy casualties, then vanished again like smoke up a winter chimney. He didn't notice that they were moving steadily north, and even if he had he could never have dreamed why they were, though Fontana was directing them.

Then one day weeks later he finally got the break he'd prayed for when Dark Eyes came upon a single set of fresh tracks in the snow early that morning. Kyle had been out on his own scouting their backtrail, then turned and started back for the hidden camp, but the Cheyenne had cut his tracks less than an hour later. When he returned to camp he mimicked and gestured until the general finally understood he'd found something important, but there was no one left but an orderly, the cook, and the mule driver, so he told the orderly where he was going and to send anyone that came back in as quick as possible. Then the two sped out of camp.

When they reached the tracks they headed up canyon toward a plateau threaded by a tiny, snow-melted creek meandering across its top, and just as they leveled out Dark Eyes caught sight of Fontana half a mile ahead out in the open and instantly sent his pony into a clattering run, spray flying, as he thundered down the waterway, a killing shout of challenge rising in his throat, while Whitehead screamed to no avail for him to come back.

Suddenly, Kyle heard the war cry and yanked Snow Ball around, surprised to see the fast-approaching red man bearing down on him, but he responded by kicking the black and white horse into a thundering run to meet him. As they pounded closer the Cheyenne leaned low in the saddle and leveled his rifle as Fontana waited until the last possible moment, then quickly swung under Snow Ball's neck firing from that position as Dark Eyes' bullet missed over the top, but his sliced into the Indian pony bringing it down kicking and screaming into a wall of water, throwing the red man over its head to land stunned for a moment until he finally regained his senses, wildly looking around for his lost rifle.

In a flash the white man leaped from his

horse to face the sinewy warrior as both pulled razor-sharp knives circling each other, parrying and thrusting for an opening until Dark Eyes suddenly charged in, slashing Kyle's buckskin wide open at the chest. Both men came together, each grabbed the other's knife hand as they twisted and jerked trying to gain the upper hand, until both lost their balance on icy snow and went down in a pool of water rolling over and over as each tried to ride atop the other and plunge their blade deep.

Finally, Kyle slowly forced the Cheyenne over, inch by inch, while he pinned his knife hand behind his back twisting it free and slamming his body weight down until the red man went under the water fighting furiously to surface and get a lung full of life giving air, but could not. He sucked in a quick gulp and forced him deeper, the drowning man struggling wildly but locked in his deathly grip until his struggles became more and more feeble, ending as a tiny stream of bubbles rose to the surface then stopped.

Slowly, Kyle pulled himself up gasping for air, wiping water from his eyes only to see a second rider bearing down on him pistol in hand, the whiskery face of General Whitehead desperate in one last ditch effort to finish off his hated foe, while he spun around looking for a rifle. There! Just a few yards away, the stock stuck up out of the snow. He lunged for it, slamming the action open and plunging his hand into soaked buckskins to find a cartridge and fumble it into the chamber, shooting from the hip as the general galloped in firing simultaneously.

Whitehead screamed in pain and tumbled from the horse to land in the pool in a shower of spray, rolling over grabbing at the leg wound, while pulling himself toward the bank. Fontana advanced, rifle in hand, until he stood literally over the top of the petrified man.

"Don't... don't kill me! For the love of God remember you're still a white man too. Please don't, I'm begging you, I'm wounded, my leg!"

He held the rifle over his head like a war club, looking down at the pathetic man who'd chased him and the Utes for so long only to come down to this. Slowly he lowered the weapon, fighting his own pent up rage, then tossed it into the snow.

"Kill you? Yes, that's what I meant to do you pathetic bastard, but now I'm not. I want you to suffer just like you've made the Utes suffer. I want you to feel that pain that goes right down to the bone, and I want it to stay there! You've lost the war whether you know it or not. Dull Knife's people will be safely across the border into Canada in another two days and there won't be a thing you can do about it. And you know what's going to happen to you, huh? When the men back in Washington that sent you here realize you've lost this war, held peace talks that were a lie even before they got started, then learn the Utes have escaped out of the country, plus the dozens of men you've got killed under your command, they'll finish you off quicker than a Ute arrow. They'll strip you of everything you've got or ever will have and run you out of the army. Kill you? I don't have to now. You've already done that to yourself. You're finished Whitehead. Washed up. Done!"

He started toward his horse, as the general rolled over in pain and panic watching him go.

"Wait! You're not going to leave me here to die like this, are you? Come back, do you hear, come back!"

Kyle mounted and rode back looking down on the water-soaked officer.

"You're not going to die, not with a leg wound, it might rot off though in time. But first tie your belt over it and start crawling back the way you came. Someone will find you today, tomorrow, maybe the day after that, but you won't die. That would be too easy."

He reined the horse around and left him lying there still calling for him to help until finally he could hear his pleas no longer.

That afternoon Quiet Moon was cleaning the knife wound as he related the story to Dull Knife and several other chiefs gathered around him.

"Do not wait. Keep your people moving for the border until you get over it safely," he advised his old friend.

"Yes, we must go, and you must ride even with your wound," the chief answered.

"No, Dull Knife. Quiet Moon and I will not go to Canada with you. I will not leave my country because of men like this Whitehead. We have a thousand miles of mountains to find a place where we can finally stop, build a log home, and raise a family in peace. That is what I mean to do. That is what you and your people have taught me to do. Such a place will keep us safe and happy. We will meet again, and may the Great Spirit always ride with you until we do."

The chief put his hand on Kyle's shoulder and for just an instant his eyes misted over then cleared as he stepped back.

"The Spirit already rides with you, Font-ana. Wovokwa has made it so."

As the Utes mounted up and pulled their

pack horses into line, Kyle and Quiet Moon stood watching them go, as he pulled her close smiling down.

"It's time for us to leave too."

He kissed her lightly on the forehead, and just as he'd promised, before the coming summer faded into another crisp fall, they found their hidden valley and had the new log home ready for three.

F ISB
Isberg, Art
Fontana /
c2002.

L M

J